Books by

The Be...

One Breath, One Bullet
Dominant Predator
Powerless
Falling, One by One
Strength of the Rising Sun

Sexy Snax

Someday It Will Be

Anthologies

Semper Fidelis

Single Titles

An Immoveable Solitude
Anomaly

An Immoveable Solitude

ISBN # 978-1-78651-890-3

©Copyright S.A. McAuley 2016

Cover Art by Posh Gosh ©Copyright 2016

Interior text design by Claire Siemaszkiewicz

Pride Publishing

Published in 2016 by Pride Publishing, Newland House, The Point, Weaver Road, Lincoln, LN6 3QN, United Kingdom.

Printed and bound in Great Britain by Clays Ltd, St Ives plc

1

AN IMMOVEABLE SOLITUDE

S.A. MCAULEY

Dedication

To the friends, both vintage and new, who have held me together over the last year. There may be thousands of miles or competing commitments between us, but my love for you all will never be muted by time or distance. Thank you.

AN IMMOVEABLE SOLITUDE

S.A. MCAULEY

Dedication

To the friends, both vintage and new, who have held me together over the last year. There may be thousands of miles or competing commitments between us, but my love for you all will never be muted by time or distance. Thank you.

Chapter One

The boat pitched from side to side as the deckhands struggled to lower the rattling cage against the hull. The sky was a cloudless indigo blue, and the stars were beginning to blink out in rings as sunrise pushed past the horizon. The air was unseasonably warm, which lowered the chances of this being a productive trip, but I wasn't going to complain. I loved summers in the Cape.

The waters of Van Dyks Bay were generally erratic, consistent in their inconsistency, and there were days I wanted to ignore the weather and wave report and just chance it, setting sail for Dyer Island without planning for what to expect. But this was our boat, our company, and we had a reputation that ensured us a steady stream of tourists.

"Oy! Hash! We need help securing the lines out here, hey?"

Abraham's voice called to me from the stern, where he and two of the deckhands pulled at the ropes used to fasten the cage to the side of the boat. The waves were too strong for divers to climb in just yet, but the wind was slowly dying and soon the pitch of the boat would turn to a slow, hypnotic roll. I left the tiny wheelhouse and helped them tie off the lines, relishing the salt spray that hit each time the boat bottomed out on a wave.

We struggled to secure the cage, and Abraham switched to Afrikaans as we worked. It was my second language, but the mother tongue for most of our crew, and when things became tense, as they did now, the tourists wouldn't understand one word we said to each other. The cage finally settled into the grooves worn into the hull from countless trips, and we fastened it tightly. Behind us, the divers talked nervously with each other, surveying the bay with suspicion, fear, excitement, or a mix of all three. They were already clad in thick wetsuits, masks hung around their necks or gripped tightly in fists. Abraham tugged at the ropes, checking them before turning to me and nodding.

"Let's give it another ten," I replied to the question he hadn't asked. "I'd like it to be a bit calmer."

I stopped to chat up the group of divers on my way to the wheelhouse. We had ten on board today, a full charter. As usual, it was a mix of nationalities and ages — six women and four men on an escorted tour of South Africa. The women today were especially flirtatious, and like any smart captain looking to see his business grow, I took the time to talk with each of them before moving on. Kerry liked to tease me that I enjoyed this part of my job a little too much.

I wore my usual blue and silver board shorts hung low on my hips, with feet and chest bare. I leaned down to speak intimately to the women, my smile flashing, my laugh genuine. My blond hair, just a touch on the long side, fell into my eyes and one of the ladies looked as if she wanted to push it back. I never discouraged it if they tried. I gave my excuses, begging off with the list of duties I had to complete. I pointed at Abraham and told them my boss made me work too hard. Abraham grinned and shook his head — he'd seen this too many times. Yet he still laughed, because both of us knew who the boss really was even though, at twenty-seven, I didn't look old enough to have my own company.

More importantly, Abraham knew I wasn't interested in any of them. No matter how free, easy or beautiful they were. I had a gorgeous man, my partner in every sense of the word, waiting for me back at our shop.

Nothing about me proclaimed my sexuality. I'd never been loud about being gay. Most days, it was the least of what defined me. But I'd never hidden it either. For some, my choice to live with my sexual orientation as secondary, like every straight person had the pleasure of doing, was unsettling. So they made assumptions when it would've been easier to ask. But for most, especially the tourists, I was little more than eye candy. Someone pleasant-looking to flirt with when away from home.

The nervous anticipation of the divers relaxed as the winds died and the waves settled the boat into a gentle sway. The sun crested over the mountains to the east, chasing the rest of the stars away. Abraham gave his standard greeting and instructions before the first divers dropped into the cage. The energy of the tourists was palpable, pulling smiles from the tired crew.

We'd all been up for hours already, prepping the boat and supplies, and performing equipment checks. This moment—when Abraham, with a twitch of his lips, asked the inevitable question, "Who wants to go first?"— was my second favorite part of the workday. Nervous laughter skittered between the tourists, and Dominick, our videographer, circled them, capturing their reactions for a personalized DVD we would sell to them after the trip. Today, it was an American who stepped forwards, a goofy grin plastered across his face. He immediately put the rest of the tourists at ease as he joked about who would get his wife if he didn't make it out.

I leaned against the helm and pulled out my cell. A green light blinked at the corner and I flipped it open to read the text.

Howzit?

I chuckled. Three years after his arrival in South Africa and Kerry still hadn't mastered the basic slang. He'd attempted it enough times that I knew he was asking how the charter was going, but the actual meaning of what he'd asked was, 'How are you?'

Lekker, was my one-word reply—*excellent*. We both spent so much time dealing with tourists that we usually had to curb the use of slang. But when it was just the two of us, jokes about the differences between his Irish English and my South African English were common.

I heard gasps and a scattering of loud curses and knew the first great white had been sighted. I peeked out of the wheelhouse to where the deckhands were tossing a fish head into the water. They dragged it back to the boat, drawing the shark closer to the cage. My cell pinged.

I can't drag my ass out of bed.

He was lying. I'd heard his footsteps on the wood floors, walking from the bedroom into the shower, as I'd left early this morning. He would be in the shop now, hunched over his desk, coffee cup in hand, his black hair most likely disheveled from running his fingers through it while he reconciled the monthly accounts. His work today wouldn't be complicated, he was too organized for that, but it would be tedious and that drove Kerry mad. He needed to be constantly entertained, and I favored the days I spent discovering new ways to keep him occupied and interested.

It's right where I want it, hey? I texted back.

The tourist group was all smiles now, enthralled with the gigantic beast cutting lazily through the water around them. Selling the DVDs was going to be easy today. Abraham and the deckhands had the divers taken care of, the water had calmed to a leisurely roll and the heat from the sun was tempered by a gentle breeze from the south. Newborn seal pups barked from the island off our bow. It was the birth of these young that had attracted the great whites back to Dyer Island and Van Dyks Bay despite the warmer waters, driving larger tourist groups our way to the point where we'd added a second boat and hoped to receive government approval for a third next year.

If you don't want your books to balance this month, Erik Hash, was his response.

He was using my full name. Not a good sign. I typed

back, *Frustrated already?*

He replied before I could look up.

I'd rather be on the boat.

I let out a low whistle. If he wanted to be on the boat more than in the shop, that meant he was more than frustrated. Kerry hated the sharks as much as I loved them. I'd met him three years ago when he'd walked onto my uncle's boat with his sister, Kelle, in tow, and I'd known then I would do anything to have him. It took me one day to get him into my bed, but almost a year before I knew he loved me as much as I loved him. Kerry and Kelle were only supposed to stay in the Cape for a week, then move on to Durban, over to Johannesburg and eventually into Botswana. After our first night together, Kerry decided not to leave Van Dyks Bay and Kelle reluctantly stayed on.

Worry lines creased my forehead as I tried to formulate a response. Kerry had been more distant than usual the last couple of days. I didn't expect him to be overtly emotional anytime — it just wasn't him. He was reserved, calm and introverted, the opposite of me, but lately he'd been more withdrawn than usual. I knew he was joking when he said he would rather be on the boat, but I read the underlying annoyance in that statement and I doubted it had anything to do with reconciling the finances. Kerry was working through something and I couldn't shake the feeling that it was bigger than he was letting on.

A collective gasp came from outside the wheelhouse and I grinned, an old joy filling me with each satisfied shriek that erupted from the deck, pulling my thoughts away from Kerry. I felt the boat pitch as the thundering footsteps of the divers followed the shark from aft to stern. It was rare that I made a trip out near Dyer Island without spotting one of the apex predators, but my excitement never waned, and my admiration for their ancient power and beauty never faltered. I was seven years old again each time I connected

9

with the black eyes of these stunning creatures.

What was I doing sequestering myself in the wheelhouse? There was nothing I could do for Kerry until the charter was done. We were on the sharks. I threw my cell into the pocket of my hoodie hung by the door, and stepped out onto the deck. There were two divers in the cage, three standing where it was anchored next to the boat, and two on the bow. Feet shuffled above my head on the second level of the boat where the rest of the divers were chatting happily as they clicked off pictures.

Abraham sidled up next to me, put his hand on my shoulder and squeezed affectionately. His bone-white teeth stood out against the deep blackness of his skin and a jovial smile told me it was a good sighting. The silver streaks he'd developed in his hair over the last two years made him even more handsome.

"How big?"

"Almost four meters," Abraham said, pointing at the shark on the aft side. "There's a three-meter juvenile creeping around as well."

We made our way behind the cage, where a deckhand tossed chum into the water, bribing the sharks to stay with our boat. There were two other companies doing the same bait-and-view routine with their own tourists so we had to keep the sharks occupied or risk losing them to one of the boats that sat a respectable distance away. I peered into the water as I saw the large shadow draw closer. I slid my polarized glasses over my eyes to block out the glare of sun on the waves and felt my breath hitch when the larger one came into view.

The sides of the shark were scarred from the number of mating seasons it had been through, the twisted patchwork of white a testament to its age. It cut gracefully through the water past the cage, ignoring the divers in the cage that were pushing as far back against the metal as possible, and yet it was obvious the shark was aware of everything happening around it. It had decided we weren't a threat long before it showed up alongside the boat. These creatures were cunning, intelligent and ancient. I knew the black of their eyes almost as well as the green of Kerry's.

The deckhand pulling the fish yanked it closer to the cage and the water surged as the juvenile crashed toward the floating fish head. The divers next to the cage jumped back with a cry of surprise, while the deckhands, Abraham and I laughed until we were nearly crying. We'd seen the shadow underneath the water as the smaller one moved in. I put my arms around the shoulders of two of the divers at the side of the boat. The petite wife of the American man pulled me closer. Her wetsuit was soaked since she'd just exited the cage.

"You see that bro over there with the video camera?" I pointed them toward Dominick so he could get a good shot of their faces after the surprise. "He's much more dangerous than the juvenile softie out there."

Dominick winked, and they twittered and blushed.

"See, I told you. Sharks are incredibly evolved predators, but you shouldn't fear them. They are shy, deliberate hunters and will rarely attack except when hunting. They will never attack the cage. Dom, on the other hand, you need to watch those teeth."

Before I could slip my arms from around their shoulders, the American woman looked at me in awe. Her teeth chattered. "I don't know whether to be frightened or amazed. You really love them, don't you? The sharks?"

"I do. There is more to be amazed of than frightened of. Listen to Abraham. He'll sell you."

I excused myself and left my co-captain to do his work. While my brain was filled with all kinds of arcane and useless trivia about sharks and their appearances on TV and in movies, Abraham had been a part of my uncle's research crew for years and could answer the important questions about shark biology and habits. Turning this part over to him was also carefully choreographed after our years of working together. I had a tendency to spout off about the evil that was TV's *Shark Week* if given half a chance. Okay, any chance. But it also gave me time to do what I really loved to do, which was watch the sharks.

I sat in the stern with the deckhands and cut up chum. It was the perfect vantage point to watch the juvenile great white stay a deferential distance from the larger shark, which only circled back once the divers had calmed down and a fresh bucket of blood was dumped into the water. I watched the shark until I felt an itch to check on Kerry.

Back in the wheelhouse, I pulled out my cell and texted, *Okay?*

I stared at the phone, waiting for a reply. I could picture him trying to think how to respond, typing something then erasing it. I closed my eyes and paid attention to the rolling of the waves beneath the boat, letting them rock me. The sun pouring through the wheelhouse window onto my shoulders and face, warm salt air filtering in through the open windows and the rhythmic sound of the waves against the hull helped calm my worry over Kerry. I didn't know how long I stood there, mesmerized and half asleep, before my cell pinged again.

Just need more coffee. And your ass back in bed.

Only a couple of more hours and I would be happy to oblige him on the second part. Because getting off the boat and coming home to Kerry, even after three years, was still my favorite part of the day.

* * * *

As soon as we docked, Abraham took the tourists into the shop to sell them the DVDs and hopefully pick up a couple of donations for the local great white conservation society. The deckhands and I cleaned up the boat and equipment, making sure it would be ready for another early-morning dive tomorrow. During summer, our high season despite the decreased likelihood of seeing sharks

12

because of warmer water, we operated seven days a week. It was a brutal schedule, but one of the reasons we were so successful. As soon as we were done on the boat, I checked in with Kelle to make sure her charter had gone okay before heading to the shop.

"Who's the kid working on the ropes?" I stood at the back door, talking to Kerry through the screen while he worked on the books. On the dock between our two boats, a teenager who was too thin, with dull brown hair and a pinched face, hunched awkwardly over a pile of ropes. He was working the knots out and coiling them back into a manageable pile. It was a task Abraham usually farmed off to one of the hands after we brought the boats back in each day. Abraham was nowhere in sight, and neither were any of our deckhands.

"Charlie."

I raised my eyebrows and looked at Kerry questioningly through the door, but he didn't acknowledge me or continue talking.

"And?"

"What, mate?"

I eyed the kid suspiciously. He was staring into the mound as if it were a snake pit and he couldn't find a safe place to put his hand. His eyebrows were drawn down sharply, making his face appear even gaunter than my initial impression. His clothes were worn, nearly transparent in places, but still neat.

"What is Charlie doing touching my ropes?"

Kerry smiled as he kept entering numbers into the computer. "I hired him on today."

"Ag, man, you're joking?"

"I'm not."

"And you decided we needed someone else why?"

"We don't. He needed us."

I stopped, immediately backing off. Kerry couldn't bear to see any person or animal suffering. It was only because of my insistence, and our crazy work hours, that our house

13

wasn't filled with stray cats and dogs. He still managed to convince me to foster anything that happened upon our doorstep until a shelter or family could take them in. I couldn't say no to him. That didn't keep me from being put off every time he brought something new home. And this one was far more than an alley cat.

I took a deep breath and reined in my temper as I ran my fingers through my hair, pulling it back from my face. I watched Charlie steadily work through the pile that was turning into a neat coil at his side. He must have felt my eyes on him, because he lifted his head and tentatively raised a hand in greeting. I mirrored the gesture and offered a smile. Charlie didn't smile back, but the slump of his shoulders lessened and he turned back to his work. If Kerry had taken him on this quickly it only meant one thing.

"He's gay."

"Aye, that he is." Kerry emphatically hit the enter key and clicked off the monitor before turning his chair in my direction. "Parents booted him six months ago. He's been on his own since."

"Legal?" I asked. Kerry knew I wasn't asking if he was legal to work. That was easy enough to get around in South Africa.

"He is."

There was hesitancy in his voice that only I or his sister would have picked up. I raised an eyebrow. "How recently?"

"Turned eighteen yesterday."

I sighed.

"I'm not much older, Erik," he reminded me.

"It's not the same and you know it," I spat out without thinking. I bit down on my tongue to keep from saying anything else and tried to see this from Kerry's point of view. It was easy for me to forget Kerry had only been nineteen when we met, and was just about to turn twenty-two now. I, on the other hand, was the old man in the relationship at twenty-seven.

I remembered how scary our first months together were for Kerry. He'd barely acknowledged to himself that he was gay, let alone anybody outside his family. He was petrified of anyone finding out, scared of the prejudice he knew he would face. And both of us knew his fears were completely legitimate, especially in Africa. There had been nothing I could say or do to reassure him. It had taken time and trust, and finally the friendship and acceptance of our friends in the Cape had helped him believe he was safe in Van Dyks Bay. But the process had been hard on both of us, and we'd had each other to fight through it. Charlie had no one.

Kerry was right. Charlie did need us more than we needed him. It was tough enough making it on your own, even more so for gay men in Africa. I pushed through the door and knelt at Kerry's feet, taking his hand into mine. I entwined our fingers and kissed the back of his hand. Kerry watched me carefully. He was looking for the tell that would let him know if I was going to yell or give in.

"Where's he going to bunk?"

Kerry squeezed my hand and sat back in his chair, but kept his fingers knitted with mine. "I offered him the second bedroom, but he wouldn't take it. I imagine he'll take the efficiency here."

I nodded. That would work well. It couldn't hurt having someone watch over the shop and boats either.

"I'll see you two at dinner." I patted his hand and pushed up, heading for the front to find Abraham.

"That's it?" he called after me.

"Yeah, baby, that's it. I trust you. Your heart is never in the wrong place." I stepped out of the office and clicked the door shut quietly. I had complete faith in Kerry. He didn't make decisions lightly. If he thought taking this kid on was a good idea, I would stand by him.

In the year since he'd taken over as our operations manager, every instinct of his had been spot on and we were making more money now than my uncle ever had. I waited at the back of the shop as Abraham chatted with

15

the last of the tourists, trying to gently move them toward the door, turning down offers to join them at the bar. Every now and then we accepted those offers, but our schedule was packed this week.

The years at sea were beginning to show on Abraham. I had thought him an old man when I was a child and he worked for my uncle. Now that he was my employee, I knew the truth. Abraham was a very old man and the best co-captain I could've hoped for. With my parents and uncle now passed on, he, Kerry and Kelle were my family.

The group called out goodbyes as they pushed happily into the warm summer day. Abraham locked the door behind them, turned to me with a wide smile and said in Afrikaans, "All of them bought the DVD."

"*Lekker*. Dominick was a great investment." I helped him shove the chairs back into place and tidy the waiting room.

"You met Charlie?" Kelle came through the door to the efficiency in the back, her tone not questioning but accusatory.

Abraham finished straightening up and got out of the room as fast as he could. I didn't blame him. Kelleigh and Kiernan Callaghan were 'Irish twins', siblings born ten months apart, but they couldn't have been more different. While Kerry was beloved by my staff, Kelle was viewed as a bulldog on a flimsy leash. It was the reason Abraham worked on my boat and not Kelle's.

"In a way," I answered, trying not to sound irritated.

"I don't know about this."

"You wouldn't," I said under my breath. Apparently not low enough for her to miss it.

"What the bloody fuck does that mean?"

I put my hands on the back of a folding chair and leaned on it. "Have some faith in your brother, yeah?"

"My brother has too much faith in others."

I cringed. That was a jab meant just for me. She followed on my heels as I went out the front door. It seemed we weren't done talking.

"I'm sorry, Hash," she said unexpectedly and I stopped to let her catch up to me. "I don't know why my first reaction is to get snippy with you."

I'd never understood it either. We could barely be in the same room without sniping at each other. Our relationship was bipolar at best, swinging in dramatic swoops from high to low. *High.*

"Are you coming to dinner?"

"No, I have class." She opened her car door and I crossed the garden heading for the house I shared with Kerry. Her voice stopped me. "Erik?" *Low*. Only Kerry was allowed to call me Erik.

"Kelle?" I responded with as much disdain as I could muster.

"This isn't a smart decision."

"It's not your decision to make."

"It won't end well."

I threw my arms up and laughed. "How do any of us know what the ending will be? Right, Kelle belle?" *Sarcastic mocking low*. Only Kerry was allowed to use the rhyming nickname.

"Don't call me that."

I snickered as she pulled away in a rush.

Chapter Two

It was our day off, the first in months where I was on land and Kerry wasn't in the shop. In the weeks since Charlie had been with us, he'd proved himself to be a fast learner with a strong work ethic. With another capable hand came the opportunity for Kerry and me to get away from the business for a day, even if we never strayed farther than a couple of miles away from our shop or house.

Kerry continued to stew on something, becoming more emotionally withdrawn than usual. And I pretended not to notice how distant he was. I'd learned years ago that he had to work problems out himself or he'd never be happy with whatever decision he was trying to make. Kelle had laid off the kick-Charlie-out campaign but kept a much closer eye on Kerry. She came around more for dinner, on her best behavior most of the time, because she knew Kerry would only put up with so much of us bickering.

Today, it was just Kerry and me.

I coaxed him out of bed long after the sun rose, a rarity in itself for us. We maneuvered around each other in the small kitchen, making a proper breakfast for once instead of having a rushed bowl of cereal or toast and jam. Kerry had gone shopping the day before, picking up bacon, blood sausage, fresh tomatoes, eggs and mushrooms and was showing off his prowess with a knife and spatula.

Anything outside of opening a can of beans was way out of my comfort zone and I sat at the counter watching Kerry work. He sliced the tomatoes into thick stacks and set them next to a pan to fry once the bacon was done. He whipped the eggs, using warmed cream instead of milk to froth them up. The smell of sizzling butter, sausage and onions filled the kitchen. Above everything that competed for my attention, my senses were tuned to Kerry—his sun-sweet scent, the faint touch of his skin as he brushed past me, the tuneless song he hummed as he chopped and sautéed. It was overwhelmingly sexy.

He turned to me, his eyes clearer than I'd seen them in weeks, and he winked. I groaned and dropped my head to the counter in defeat. He was devastatingly handsome.

"You okay, baby?" he chuckled as he smoothed my hair back from my face and ran his thumb across my jaw. He continued to laugh when I pressed into his hand and shook my head. I could feel his laugh through the counter and his hand. It rumbled around me, ratcheting up my awareness of just how close he was and how free we were for the day. I turned my head and took his thumb into my mouth, circling my tongue around the sides and up to the tip as I slowly let it slide out.

"Fuck," Kerry whispered, his Irish accent drawing the word out sensually. He shut off the gas burners and tossed the pans to the side. "Breakfast later," was all he said before pulling me off the bar stool to the kitchen floor. He kissed up my neck and pulled at my earlobe with his teeth. His breath was hot against my neck and my skin flushed just from this light touch. His body pressed tightly against mine, and his knees urged my legs apart as he slowly ground against me.

His cock stiffened next to mine, torturing me with the hard press of his length. I pushed at our waistbands, hooking my thumbs in to pull them down, but Kerry pulled my hands away, sat up and straddled my waist. I groaned in frustration and grabbed on to his hips as I thrust up. He chuckled again, then leaned down and lifted my arms above my head, binding my wrists with one hand. He kissed me, slowly at first, his tongue sliding gently across my bottom lip. I moaned into his mouth, lost to the feeling of his generous lips gliding over my lips. His grip on my wrists tightened as the kiss deepened. I was starving for him. I hadn't realized how long it had been since we'd lost ourselves in each other. Work, life, family...it all added up and got in the way. I breathed him in, basking in Kerry touching me body and soul.

* * * *

After hot sex, a cold breakfast and a warm shower, I was molten laziness. I dragged him back into bed and onto my chest where he fell asleep again, curled into my side. I ran my fingers through his hair as it dried into a tangle of black curls. Any day now he would shave it down again.

His breath was even, light, and his eyes danced under the lids as he dreamt. I pulled him tighter into my arms and kissed his head, every part of me aware of Kerry's presence, awash with love, hope and protectiveness that I couldn't begin to find the right words to describe. I knew he relied on me, thought of me as the more intelligent of the two of us, and it confounded me he couldn't, or didn't, see that his value to me was more than want or desire. I *needed* Kerry.

I didn't remember falling asleep, but when Kerry's voice pried me awake I realized I'd been in the midst of a dream that left me feeling uneasy, even though the images dissolved at the first whisper of his breath on my neck.

His mouth skated down my chest, his tongue circled each nipple as I arched into him, then trailed down to envelop my dick with his full lips. I moaned, going from asleep to unnervingly awake and soft to painfully hard in a second. I didn't last long, but Kerry knew I wouldn't. He was brilliant at surprise attacks. He would do this and leave me panting, brainless and unable to resist his next request. Even as I knew it was happening, I was too blissful and disconnected to care.

I groaned in protest when, after a considerate recovery time, Kerry used his advantage to coax me into a long run up the hills around the bay. Kerry's body was built for running. His legs were long, his steps fluid and graceful. I, on the other hand, was neither light on my feet nor quick. I loved rugby for a reason. It was a game I could dominate in. I had great balance and could get down to a lower point than most men. I knew how to tackle at the waist and still maintain control and forwards momentum, skills that Kerry teased me were more useful in the bedroom than the field.

Regardless, as we ran the trail heading up the ridge, Kerry pulled ahead of me early and stayed there, doubling back every ten minutes to make sure I was still behind him. I could see the tension lifting each time he reappeared at my side.

I loved being out here with him. I didn't know why the thought hadn't occurred to me earlier. We hadn't been outside the city in months. Even though Kerry was a dive master, his element was the earth. I chastised myself for not remembering that Kerry needed the land like I needed the water. I got my fix on the bay or, on a really good day, taking a charter past Dyer Island and out into the open ocean. But Kerry was stuck inside most days, tied to his computer, phone and the shop. I'd neglected a part of him that was just as vital to his survival as food or air.

I crested over the last hill and found Kerry standing on a rock at the edge of the drop-off. He stood with his back to me, hands on his hips, chest rising and lowering with minimal effort as he caught his breath. He'd probably run twice the distance I had and he looked more energized than when we started.

He turned, flashed me a beaming smile and beckoned me to join him on the rock. He didn't put his arm around me when I stood next to him. That wasn't Kerry. But the expression on his face was one of utter happiness and I could overlook just about anything to see that contentment every day, especially after how withdrawn he'd been for the last three weeks.

"I forgot how much I love this place," he said, an air of wonder tingeing his words.

I tried to imagine how Kerry saw Van Dyks Bay. To me,

this vantage point made the city look foreign. I was used to seeing it from the water.

"What do you see when you look out there?"

Kerry cocked his head to the side and thought for a moment before he replied. "I see our home and our shop. I see the water, stretching on for miles. I see the road heading out of town, the road most of the tourists traverse as they become one-day residents in your shark cage. But most of all, I see how expansive this place truly is. I forget that. We're almost at the end of the world here. When I first came here there was something very seductive about that."

I understood exactly what he was saying. "I'm sorry I haven't paid more attention to what you need, Kerry."

A darkness passed over his face. "Never, Erik. Don't ever think that. You've given me more than I could have thought to ask for."

I looked into his eyes, trying to see what it was he was hiding from me, because I was sure now there was something. "Are you sure? These last couple weeks…"

Kerry cut me off. "Not here, Erik. Not now."

His face was hard, completely devoid of the happiness I'd seen only a heartbeat earlier. He showed nothing, betrayed nothing. This was a Kerry I rarely saw and would have done anything to never see again. Emotionless, withdrawn. I studied him for only a fraction of a second, long enough to know that it was time to get him moving again. "Let's head back."

On the way down the hill Kerry took off and didn't return to check on me. I kept my distance and let him run. At the bends in the dirt path, I saw him down the hill, shoulders back, head held high, each step effortless but deliberate. As we descended, the ease gradually returned to his step. He took the shortcut toward the beach, looking back to see if I was following.

I jogged to catch up to where he stood waiting for me. Yes, Kerry and I had been through our ups and downs, perhaps even more so since we lived and worked together.

But Kerry's almost complete emotional withdrawal over the last few weeks scared me. Kerry was working through something big, something he didn't want to talk to me about. I searched his face as I approached.

He stared out at the ocean, his body turned away from me, but the expressionless mask was gone. My shoes crunched against the rocks at the edge of the road and his head snapped back as if he were just remembering I was there. But his easy smile returned, pushing any remnants of the clouds away, and he knelt down to unlace his *tekkies*.

We left our shoes by the road and walked along the beach. Van Dyks Bay was surrounded by rocks. Tourists who came here for the first time expected sandy beaches and were shocked to discover a harsh, craggy landscape. This was a tough land, constantly assaulted by the tides from Antarctica. I'd grown up with this terrain, in a tiny house not far from my uncle's shop.

I admired the way the sweat and salt spray ran in thin rivulets down Kerry's tall, toned body, his skin just beginning to take on that golden hue I never would've thought possible on an Irishman. He was beautiful, stunningly so, and had a heart to match. He had everything going for him, yet his shyness kept him on the periphery when he deserved to be the center of attention.

Kerry kept a friendly distance, and I knew it wasn't because of what I'd said on the cliff. His smile indicated he had moved past that. This was because he was unwilling to let his guard down in public, even though everyone in town knew we were together. Whenever we left the house or shop, he maintained a respectable distance between us. Whether it was the fear of other people's actions and judgments, or because he didn't want to flaunt our relationship in front of those who might be uncomfortable with it, I didn't know. Either way, I tried not to let it sting.

He turned his head to toss a teasing comment back to me, giving me that smile, his eyes gleaming, and I ached with love for him. He would come around eventually. I just had

23

to give him time. Time didn't cost me anything when I had him at my side.

The sun beat down on us, heavy but not oppressive, and the waves crashed against the rocks in a rhythmic ebb and rush, drowning out the sounds of the highway behind us. Kerry stooped to study a tide pool. The ridges of his shoulder muscles flexed as he dipped his hand into the water. I wanted to get down next to him, to rest my chin against the hollow between his shoulder and neck, to breathe him in as I was able to do behind closed doors, but I knew he wouldn't allow me to do that out here.

Then his hand was in mine and he was pulling me down beside him. His arm wrapped around me, and his gaze speared me, keeping me still despite the automatic urge to pull back, shock written across my face.

"Relax, baby," he teased and he kissed me.

His lips barely touched mine, but I felt the softness of them in every nerve of my body. It was the first time he'd ever kissed me outside our house or the shop. And I knew that whisper of a kiss would be seared into my memory forever. Fingers slick with warm salt water, he placed something in my palm. He curled my hand into a fist, kissed me below the ear and took off down the rocks, his chuckle rumbling back to me.

I watched him jog away, felt the blush rising in my cheeks as a smile spread across my face, and I opened my palm to find a shark tooth. It was brilliant white, a perfect triangle, the serrated edges catching on my skin. I'd made the mistake when we were drinking one night of confessing to Kerry that he reminded me of the great whites — beautiful, strong, untamed, intelligent, dangerously focused and skittish. He'd taken every opportunity since then to tease me about it.

After a day of so many highs marred by the shortest of low moments, this felt like a peace offering. My Kerry, my shark, presenting a piece of himself to me.

"I just worry for you, Kerry."

I heard Kelle's voice in the living room as I stepped out of the bedroom and started downstairs. There was an edge to Kelle's words that I wasn't used to hearing when she talked to Kerry. She was the elder sibling, if only by ten months, and took that position more seriously than she needed to, but was never heavy-handed. She was Kerry's most adamant guard, and would have taken my throat out if she knew I often likened her to a bulldog. Despite our differences, real or not, being fiercely protective of Kerry was the one thing we shared. Kerry must have done something to wave her off, because her next words were even tenser.

"Listen to me," she implored insistently. Kelle never begged, so my curiosity grew as I descended to the living room.

Kelle was on the couch next to Kerry, her feet tucked under her legs, left arm along the back and her body turned toward his. Everything about her body language said she was upset, as if she was ready to spring into action at any moment. Whether that was into Kerry's arms to force him to listen to her, or off the couch and out of the door, I couldn't tell. Kerry, on the other hand, sat back into the pillows, casually flipping the pages of a book, his feet resting on a stack of magazines on the coffee table.

"Hash, tell him to listen to his older sister."

I put my hands up in a defensive posture. It was pointless and dangerous to get between the Irish twins when they were having an argument. They were practiced in the art of digging their heels in for no good reason. And I especially wasn't going to take sides when I didn't even know what they were fighting about. My natural inclination was to side with Kerry regardless, but there had been times when Kelle and I had ended up with the same viewpoint and worked with each other to convince Kerry. Those times were few and far between. I wanted Kelle to like me, but blindly taking her position wasn't going to help my cause any.

Kerry put a bookmark in and placed the novel on his lap. He gazed coolly between Kelle and me, his lip giving a barely perceptible twitch, enough for me to know he was enjoying this.

"She wants to talk about Charlie."

I pinched the bridge of my nose. "Jesus Christ, Kelle. Let it go. Kerry made the decision. It's done, yeah?" I immediately knew I'd bought a couple more years of the silent treatment from Kelle with that one statement. She fumed, her whole body taut. The angle of her cheekbones intensified when she took in a deep breath and closed her eyes.

Kerry's upturned lip was now a victorious smirk. He'd managed to shift her anger over to me, which had probably been his plan all along. I gave him the finger and he tried to suppress a laugh. He was aware of the tension between Kelle and me. Everyone was. But he didn't pay it any heed. He was content having us both in his life, whether we were fighting or getting on. Kerry found the verbal sparring matches between Kelle and me entertaining and encouraged them when he wanted to. The bastard.

Her brown eyes flashed when she finally looked up at me. "You know as well as I do that having a young kid, gay no less, staying in your home is not going to make things any easier for Kerry."

"First of all, he's eighteen. Second," I counted my points off on my fingers, "we're both gay and everyone knows that. So no shocker there. Third, he's staying in the shop, not here. Fourth, really? You're worried about Kerry? Look at that fucker laugh at us."

Kelle gave a sideways glance at her brother who was now holding his hand up to his mouth. His whole body shook as he tried to stifle a laugh. Kelle glared.

"Fifth, fuck you. I told you weeks ago this was Kerry's decision, not yours. Get over it."

"Bloody fuck," Kerry whispered before I'd stopped talking. He knew I'd taken it one step further than I needed

26

to. He stood up and bolted for the kitchen, laughter trailing behind him. I continued to stare Kelle down even though her anger visibly rose. Her fists clenched and unclenched at her sides and I wondered if this would be the time that she took a swing at me. We'd come close enough plenty of times over the years.

I saw the gleam in her eyes before she opened her mouth and knew that whatever she said next was going to be deliberately cruel and said only to bait me, and yet that didn't take the sting away once the words were out of her mouth. "Kerry didn't want to come out and you forced that decision on him."

"Kelle!" Kerry growled a warning from the kitchen before appearing in the door. "I know I bait the two of you, but I won't let you talk to Erik like that. It's time for you to go."

Kelle's face was flaming red, her lips drawn in a thin line. Kerry pulled her into a hug she didn't fight, but she kept her arms at her side.

"Out you go," he whispered into her ear barely loud enough for me to hear, then started pushing her to the door.

Kelle stopped in front of me. "Let me say one last thing to Hash."

Kerry raised an eyebrow.

"Alone, please," she clarified. When her brother didn't move, she shrugged, her face softening. "I promise to be nice."

Kerry chuckled, gave her a kiss on the cheek, then one to me, and went back into the kitchen.

Kelle took two steps forwards until she was just inches from my face. "You and I both will die before we see any harm come to that boy. I'm not daft, I know you love him. But Kerry's been different lately..." She pursed her lips and glanced at the kitchen where we could hear Kerry moving about, preparing dinner.

She might have been going around it the wrong way, but in this fight Kelle and I were on the same side. She assumed the problem was Charlie, and I knew it wasn't. What we needed to do was work together to find out what he was hiding.

"I've noticed," I admitted.

"Then you're not as oblivious as I thought." There was relief in her voice.

I huffed in protest, but she ignored me. "Charlie is staying."

She whipped her head back around to me. "I know. I had to try. There's something. I thought Charlie might be the problem. Just..." Tears appeared in her eyes. "Watch out for him."

I'd never seen Kelle cry. She blinked and just as suddenly as the tears had appeared, they were gone.

"I'm in this for life," I said, tipping my head to Kerry, humming in the kitchen.

She laughed darkly and bit her bottom lip. "Yeah, I know."

Before I could shoot off a scathing reply, she walked out. I took a deep breath, frustrated but trying not to let my temper take over. I clicked the door shut behind her and locked it. Kerry whistled in the kitchen, cabinets and drawers sliding lightly open then almost silently shut. The lack of noise told me Kerry was in his culinary zone.

The sweetness of onions and garlic sautéing in a skillet on the stove filled the house. The faint rhythmic chop of one of his overpriced, but necessary, knives echoed each time it cut into the wood chopping block. Our kitchen was tiny by any standard, but Kerry often said all he needed to make a passable meal was a good set of knives and sturdy pots and pans. He proved that theory right on a daily basis.

The floorboards creaked as I moved. Kerry knew I couldn't resist joining him in the kitchen even if I wouldn't be of any help. I stopped to turn on his laptop and start up one of my playlists. Barber's *Adagio for Strings* rose from the tinny speakers and I leaned against the desk, elbows propped on each side of the keyboard and my head in my hands, as I reined in the frustration that had built with Kelle's visit.

She had known me for three years, and never once had I

done anything to harm her or her brother, and yet we still couldn't find more than Kerry in common. Every encounter with her was a fight—sometimes a battle, sometimes merely a skirmish—and I'd grown tired of it, but I didn't know how to make it stop. I tried calming myself down by matching my breaths to the mournful slide of violin bow against string.

"What is her problem with me?" I finally asked through clenched teeth, making sure my question was loud enough to carry to the adjoining kitchen.

Kerry laughed and I felt that coil of tension slipping. "Don't ask me, mate. You're going to have to ask her." He peeked around the corner, a wine bottle and corkscrew in his hand. "Could you pick a track that's not so melodramatic?"

I eyed him suspiciously. It was hard to believe they could be so close and never discuss me. "You're her twin. Don't you talk about me or at least have that twin mojo?"

He disappeared back into the kitchen, his voice fading behind the sound of a bubbling pot of water. "I think that's only when you share a womb. At the same time."

"Smartass," I said loud enough for him to hear, then clicked a new track—some English guy Kerry loved who droned on about his miserable life over an infectious drum beat. It was melodramatic in a pop music way, a musical compromise that instantly buoyed me as I crept up behind him at the stove.

"What are you making me?" I put my arms around his waist and laid my cheek against his back. He put a hand on mine, attempting to pull me closer while using the other to stir the pot on the stove.

"Ham and Swiss boxty."

I sighed contentedly into his shoulder. He knew how much I loved it when he cooked traditional Irish dishes and his potato pancakes were my favorite. I squeezed him tighter and thought about our last trip to Ireland, where Kerry and Kelle's mum had taught me a poem she'd sung to the twins when she cooked. I started reciting it aloud.

"Boxty on the griddle, boxty in the pan, if you can't make boxty" — Kerry chuckled and sing-songed the end with me — "you'll never get a man."

"Ma taught me well."

"Aye, she did," I answered mimicking his Irish lilt. "Colcannon?"

"Aye. I'm making that as well. But you know no self-respecting Irishman eats colcannon with his boxty?"

"Fuck it all. Colcannon is mashed potatoes, boxty is pancakes. They're different. I think I like potatoes more than you do. Beer?"

"I have one." He motioned with his head to the Heineken on the counter next to him.

I started to pull away, but he held on, put the spatula down and snaked his hand back and around my ass. He lingered there and I felt my body responding. The light was low in here, always had been even when I was a kid and this was my uncle's house, and that combined with the warmth of the stove and Kerry's body pressed against mine was enough to dispel the last fragments of anger.

"Oy! Fair warning, I'm headed inside," Charlie called from the front door.

"We're in here," Kerry answered as he gave my ass one last disappointed squeeze.

"Was that Kelle I saw driving out?" Charlie didn't look nearly as gaunt as he had that first day on our dock, but he was still awkward, stilted.

"Aye."

Charlie giggled. "Still trying to convince you to get rid of me?"

I looked at Kerry. I should have guessed he would be unwilling to keep this from Charlie. Kerry nodded as Charlie entered the room and I pulled out beers for Charlie and me.

"Don't take it too personally, yeah?" I responded. "She doesn't like me either."

"Maybe that's because you're doing her brother."

I nearly spat out my beer. Kerry had to hold onto the side of the stove to keep from falling over, he was laughing so hard. Charlie blushed and hid his smile behind his beer bottle. Every day I spent with the kid, I liked him more. He was witty, shy, careful—similar to Kerry in so many ways. He worked hard and was honest.

While I had been dubious about Charlie's sudden appearance in our lives, it was becoming more difficult to remember why I'd ever thought taking him in was a bad idea. Charlie looked to me as a mentor and I took that responsibility seriously. We sat on bar stools and watched Kerry cook. He started his tuneless humming and I knew we wouldn't have his attention again until dinner was ready.

"Howzit?"

Charlie looked down at the counter, considering. I let him think. I was fully aware it was a loaded question. When he answered, it was in Afrikaans. Even though Kerry had lived in South Africa for three years, he only spoke select phrases in Afrikaans. Since English was the primary language here, and I spoke Afrikaans fluently, he'd never had to learn. Charlie switched over to Afrikaans so Kerry wouldn't understand what he was saying. "I'm afraid that being here is causing trouble for Kerry."

My immediate response was to ask why he wasn't worried about me, but I knew why. Kerry was the one who'd taken Charlie in and it was his sister who had the big problem with it. Not to mention Charlie had been around long enough to pick up on how uncomfortable Kerry was about his sexual orientation being made known publicly, and taking in a teenage stray who was also gay brought us all more attention.

I responded in Afrikaans. "Kerry wants you here." I looked at Kerry. He was so involved in his cooking he hadn't noticed we were speaking in Afrikaans, let alone that his name had come up twice already.

"That's not my worry, yeah? *Should* I be here?"

"Yes," I answered without hesitation. Kerry had been half right when he'd said Charlie needed us. We also needed Charlie. He had slid into our lives and business effortlessly and filled a need I hadn't even known we had. Because of Charlie, Kerry and I were able to spend more time together, time I hadn't realized we were missing until it was almost too late.

Kerry was still off-kilter, but better since our day off, and we now had time away planned weeks in advance. We were going to have many more opportunities like that because of Charlie.

"You want to ask me again how I'm doing?"

I switched to English. "Howzit?"

He followed suit. "My bosses are working me to the bone."

The corner of Kerry's lip twitched. Apparently, he was listening.

"*Isit*? I bet you're sleeping great."

"*Ja*, better than I have in months."

"Cheers to that." I lifted my bottle to Charlie's. Kerry wiped his hands on the dishrag over his shoulder and picked up his Heineken. The clink of the bottles was almost lost in the sound of the sizzling frying pan and Charlie's laughter when Kerry mussed his hair affectionately. For this moment, everything felt right.

Chapter Three

"Long day."

Kerry sat on the couch, a book in his hands that he immediately shut when I pushed open our front door. "Aye, right?"

"Aye," I mocked, his presence already easing me. "'Twas a very long day." And it truly had been a tough day. Our charters had been maxed, the tourists had been antsy and only one shark had appeared during the whole four-hour trip. But now I was home with Kerry and free to toy with him for a bit. I purposefully walked past him without a look, bounded up the stairs and headed into the bathroom. I stripped down and started the shower.

"What did you make me for dinner?"

He was silent.

I grinned and stepped into the steaming water.

"Baby? You hear me? What's on the menu for tonight?"

The bathroom door squeaked on its hinges as Kerry pushed it open. His footfalls on the tile were soft, unobtrusive, almost hesitant. "You're not serious, mate?"

I stifled a laugh. "Ag, man, I'm exhausted. I need food, a drop of beer then bed."

"Sure there's nothin' you're forgetting?"

Cool air dissipated the steam surrounding me when he threw the shower curtain open, one hand on his hip, his beautiful lips pouting. He looked absolutely devastated and I started to feel guilty for teasing him. Then he saw the grin on my face and yelled at me, "You bloody fuck!"

I grabbed him by the hem of this T-shirt before he could escape and pulled him to the edge of the tub. My feet slid underneath me and I had to pull at him to keep myself from tumbling, which caused him to pitch forwards and take a step under the water. He looked down at his jeans, one leg now thoroughly soaked, and tried to glare at me, but instead broke out into one of his deep laughs. I urged him to step all the way in and he followed without protest, soaking the rest of his clothes completely. I circled my arms around his waist and leaned down to kiss his neck.

"Happy birthday, love."

He pushed hair back from my temple and kissed my forehead, lingering there until I could feel this one, simple kiss in every nerve of my body.

"You didn't really think I'd forget?"

His lips skated against my cheek as he responded, "No, I suppose not. So the party is still on?"

"A traditional *jol*. Just for you. At the beach in an hour."

He wrapped his arms around my shoulders, bringing my head against his chest. The well-worn cotton of his T-shirt was coarse compared to his water-slick skin, and I could see his breath quickening underneath the translucent cloth. I imagined stripping him down and immediately began to harden. He ran his hands down the length of my back then around my hips possessively. His touch wasn't gentle. I couldn't hold back my moan.

"Which means..." he said, his voice rumbling suggestively in my ear.

"Which means you have an hour to use me in whatever way you want, old man."

Kerry huffed. "I'm twenty-two today!"

I angled my neck to give him better access, relenting to the soft push of his lips at my collarbone. "Ag, shame, and over the hill already."

He pushed me against the wall and I shivered more from the force than the coldness of the tile behind me. There was little I loved more than when Kerry got so turned on he became overly aggressive. His clothes scratched against my skin, and the contrast between his roughness and the

34

slick tile behind me sent a shot of desire skittering through my veins. His lips brushed mine, and I tipped my head forwards to pull him into a deeper kiss. The water from the shower continued to beat down on his head and run down his cheeks as I twined our tongues together. The water was cool dropping from his lips onto my tongue, mixing seductively with the warmth of Kerry's mouth and the taste that was only him.

I undid the top button of his jeans and slid my hand inside, freeing his cock from the soaking fabric. He moaned when I gripped his head and teased the ridge with my thumb. He stepped out of his jeans, kicked them back as I peeled his T-shirt off and tossed it out of the shower. My heart sped as he stood completely naked in front of me. Three years later and he was able to make me spiral out of control with just one look, the intensity in his heavy-lidded eyes stilling me, making my body ache for his touch.

Kerry loved to seduce me.

He put his hands on the tile on either side of my head and leaned down to kiss me gently. His dick brushed against mine and I knew that Kerry was controlling even that. I put my hands on his hips as they swiveled sensuously, letting the head of his cock slide around mine and pulling it away as soon as I began to moan.

He repeated this until every part of me was on fire and I was begging for him to touch me more. Despite my pleas, Kerry continued to tease his cock against mine, breaking my control down piece by piece until my knees were shaking. Only then did he curl his head into my shoulder and kiss my neck, pressing our chests together, his hand snaking around my ass to steady me. I took both our cocks into my hand and stroked us together. The water slicked our skin as I pulled roughly, causing heat and friction that threatened to fray and snap my last tethers of control.

When he cried out, it nearly did me in. But I didn't want to finish like this.

I pushed him away and confusion flashed across his face

when I turned my back to him. I watched him over my shoulder as he put it together, his face going from confusion to understanding to uninhibited desire. I gripped the towel bar, and motioned to the shelf where I'd put a bottle of lube this morning.

"Bloody hell, Erik," he groaned. His bass voice rumbled through me and I felt my cock twitch in anticipation.

I closed my eyes, leaned my forehead on the tile and waited for him to make the next move. The water pounded my back and ran down my ass, where it teased my hole. Each second that passed was more exquisite torture as I imagined where Kerry would touch me first. I heard him take the bottle off the ledge, open it and set it back down, but still he didn't reach for me. My muscles clenched in anticipation of his fingers exploring me, his cock filling me.

He was just as excited about this game as I was. I could feel the energy pouring off him in waves as he hovered, his naked body just inches away from mine. When he finally moved closer, I tensed.

He kissed me at the crease between my ass and my thighs, first one side and then the other, his full lips sucking softly at the skin as he nipped gently again and again. I arched back into his touch as his tongue traced a line from my balls to my hole, sending jolts of pleasure racing through my body. He stood, trailing his fingertips up my thighs and along my stomach, and placed a kiss at the base of my neck just as he used his slicked finger on my rim before gently pushing it inside. He quickly added another finger and I rocked against him, the feel of him fucking me with his hand bringing me to the edge too quickly. I pulled away, not wanting to come yet.

A groan came from deep in his chest and he grabbed my ass cheek and harshly forced me back. The sensations were overpowering. I swore in Afrikaans, begging him to fuck me already, and although he could barely speak a word of it, he knew what that phrase meant.

He put his arm around my waist and guided himself

inside me in one long, slow slide. His breath in my ear was ragged from holding back his own orgasm. We rocked together, his hand pumping my cock, the muscles of his chest gliding against my back.

There was desperation every time Kerry and I fucked. We rarely made love. Maybe it was because even after all these years we still hadn't gotten enough of each other. Maybe it was that I craved his touch, demanded it. Or maybe it was the only time Kerry was truly free to let go. Whatever it was, Kerry's touch was never gentle when we fucked like this, but these were the times I knew without a doubt Kerry loved me and needed me as much as I did him.

He bit at my neck and a low growl escaped from his lips that sent me over the edge. I felt him push harder and faster into me as my body clenched around him. He yelled out when his release hit and he slammed into me, going as deep as possible. I hung onto the bar to keep us from sliding to the shower floor as we rode out the last waves.

"Now that's a happy fucking birthday, baby." Kerry kissed down my back as he collapsed.

I chuckled. "Happy fucking birthday, Kerry."

He slapped my calf muscle and lay down in the bath, throwing his arm over his eyes in exhaustion.

I sank down to my knees next to him. "Come on, old man. We have to get you ready for your party."

Kerry was already half asleep. "What party?" he whispered.

I laughed. "The *jol*? On the beach? Kelle got kudu for the grill?"

He lifted his arm and looked at me seriously for only a second before he couldn't hold out anymore and a deep chuckle rumbled through his chest. "Fuck it. I'm just going to die here."

* * * *

Lucky for us, Kerry's birthday fell during early December,

37

in the midst of a string of pleasant days. Abraham, Charlie and Kelle had set up the party behind the shop. The street was already full of cars when Kerry and I walked out our front door and around the shop. A summer breeze crested off the water and swirled around us, carrying the scents of chicken and kudu on the South African *braai*.

The choice of kudu had been all Kerry. It was one of the first meats he'd had when arriving in the Cape and he'd developed a taste for it. I personally shuddered at the thought of eating the creature that ran freely on the plains north of us, even though it was considered a delicacy.

The sun was just beginning to drop behind the hills in the west and more people arrived as we walked around. Kerry was drawn from embrace to embrace, his cheeks red from kisses by the time I got him back.

He was flushed, sated and happy. Happier than I'd seen him since our day off. There was no trace of any darkness in his eyes tonight.

Even though it was his party, Kerry immediately went for the *braai*, taking over the delicate process of cooking the kudu. He chatted at the grill with Kelle's boyfriend, a rugby player from the Cape who towered over her and was head over heels in love with her even though they'd only been together a couple of months. Charlie and Abraham sat in chairs on the dock, strings of lights strung along the railings and above them from lamp post to lamp post. They tipped their bottles to me in greeting, but kept up their conversation as I walked by. Their voices drifted past me on the wind and I could hear snippets of conversations in Afrikaans and English, the words melting and twisting into each other companionably.

I stood at the edge of the rocks, looking out over the sea of friends I'd grown up with. They had adopted Kerry as one of their own. I was lucky and I couldn't have asked for more tangible proof.

"*Lekker jol*, Kelle," I said as she sidled up next to me.

"You know you could just say 'excellent party'."

"Aye, I could, lass," I said with a wink.

"I'm not a fucking leprechaun, you know?" She drank her beer. "I just talk like one sometimes."

I spat out the bit I was drinking and looked at her dumbly. Was that a joke coming out of Kelle's mouth and not a verbal jab? It had to be a first. She smiled slyly and I laughed.

"How was it planning this with Charlie?" I smirked.

"Don't be an arse, Hash."

I held out a hand to call a truce. "For Kerry, yeah?"

The corner of her mouth twitched up and she took my hand. "Aye, for Kerry. But only tonight."

"*Ja*, I know." I drank my beer, taking in the sounds of the ocean waves hitting the shore.

"How's he doin'?"

"Still not talking about whatever it is. But better."

"You sure?"

I nodded.

"Good."

There was silence between us for a minute, then I cleared my throat. "This has been fun. Same time next year?"

I thought Kelle was going to collapse, she was laughing so hard. "Go play with your friends, Hash."

There was still a barrier between us, and I didn't know if we'd ever get past it. But I knew without a doubt that, while she didn't like me, she would never get in the way of my relationship with Kerry.

I made a circuit through the crowd, catching up with friends I hadn't seen in ages because of our hectic schedule. Someone passed a plate of food to me and I caught Kerry's eyes and gave him a thumbs up on the kudu. Even I had to admit it was delicious.

It must have been hours later that I finally pulled away to look for Kerry. I followed the torch light and drifting sound of music closer to the water. Kerry sat on a boulder, a guitar in his hands. He picked at the strings, playing a tune either I didn't recognize or he was making up as he went. I suspected Kerry was a composer of sorts and his humming and guitar playing were ways for him to work out pieces of the whole, much like how I assumed he worked out problems in his head.

I sat down on his left and kissed his shoulder. Kerry looked up at me contentedly, his eyes bright, reflecting the white lights lining the dock and the fire of the torches wedged into the rocks around him. I wanted to get lost in those eyes, to never look away, but too soon he was turning away from me, taking requests from the small group around us, as his deep bass voice took on everything from Johnny Cash to Kurt Cobain to The Killers.

As the night went on, we ended up with our backs to each other, him continuing to sing and play guitar with friends in one circle while I talked and shared stories with the group in front of me. Long after the sun set, we stayed, laughter and music twining around us, as we passed around beers and kudu jerky.

Despite it being the busy season, our boats would be grounded tomorrow. It was Kerry's birthday celebration, but it was also a gift to our crew. They needed an occasional break as much as we did, and we hadn't done anything with all of us in one place since last year. Kerry's voice reverberated in my back as it rumbled in his chest and up past those irresistible lips, and that alone was enough to keep me warm.

Eventually people began to leave as a chill settled into the air. Before long it was only Kerry and I left on the beach. He set his guitar to the side and I handed him a box.

"I told you not to get me anything, babe."

"You already know what it is. I just thought I'd give it to you tonight."

He opened the box and pulled out the shark tooth I'd had mounted onto the necklace setting he'd requested.

"Help me put it on?"

I unclasped the necklace and laid the pendant against his chest. It stood out in stark relief against the fitted black V-neck sweater he wore above faded low-slung jeans. I kissed his neck as I fastened the necklace and let it drop beneath his shirt.

"Thank you, Erik."

"Anything for you."

We huddled into each other and shared stories from the different people we'd talked to that evening. I tried to tamp down the question that kept popping into my mind as we talked, the one that had been on the tip of my tongue all night as I realized how perfect my life was.

I knew it was a dangerous question, one that was putting a whole lot of my blood in the water, just begging Kerry to take a chunk out of me, but every moment with him made my resolve drop further and I was asking it before I even realized I'd opened my mouth.

"Do you think someday that you may want to marry me, Kerry?"

I felt him stiffen. I sighed. *Teeth sinking in.*

"I said someday. I'm not asking you tonight."

He didn't answer me. *A yank at my flesh.*

"What scares you so much? The commitment? The service? Me?" The last question was squeaked out as emotion started to take over.

"I can't do this..." *Limbs gone.*

"Jesus, Kerry. Relax. I'm not asking you. Not now. I just hope that maybe...someday..."

He looked at me and a piece of me died. *Heart stopping.* His face was filled with dread. His skin went white, his eyes dulled. "I..."

I laid my head on his shoulder and rubbed his back, pushing down the tears that threatened to flood down my cheeks. I swallowed the lump in my throat, feeling it settle heavily in my stomach. "Shh, Kerry. It's okay."

"I'm sorry, Erik."

"Don't be. I know being out is hard for you. I know that. I really do."

I expected him to counter with his usual reply of me deserving better, but he stayed silent. Then he pulled me

41

into his lap and it took everything I had not to lose it. I knew Kerry wasn't ready. It was too easy to forget how young he was, in soul and body, and how real his fear of being out was to him.

I had to be grateful for every piece of himself he'd given me so far. He was skittish and more afraid than I realized. But he was here now, with me, holding me in his arms.

He sang quietly and occasionally gave me a kiss. I thought I felt a tear drop but couldn't be sure. My Kerry didn't cry. I held onto him and listened to the hypnotic crash of waves against the rocks. I breathed the salt air deeply into my lungs, letting it cleanse away the pain that spiked through me.

I didn't know how long we sat there, but when we finally stood to walk home, the night sky was so clear I could see layers upon layers of stars, pushing far out into the universe, way past where any human would ever set foot. I stood entranced, aware of what was so far away and what was right next to me. And yet it felt as if their positions should be reversed, because I was no longer sure which of them, distant galaxies or the man next to me, were more unattainable.

* * * *

A crackle. Rustling. Orange light behind my eyes. The mattress sinking beside me then bouncing back. I bit back a curse. Kerry was a restless sleeper and was often up and down. And I could sleep through everything, but not this?

Wait.

"Fuck!"

I was sitting up before I was awake. Kerry's feet pounded down the stairs, his cry echoing in my ears. Around me the room appeared to flicker, like a mirage, ribbons of fire shimmering against the ice-blue walls. I blinked, still not fully awake, trying to decide if the fire was inside the room or not. I wasn't asleep anymore, yet this couldn't be real.

What I was seeing had to be wrong. It kept me frozen in disbelief. Because Kerry had left, I knew I wasn't in danger, but something was wrong, something was on fire, and it had to be close.

The shadows in the bedroom were slowly being wiped away by an increasing glow coming through the glass block windows on the wall facing the ocean. The rippled glass warped the white-orange light as it passed through the bubbled panes, creating demonic shapes that danced frantically across the plaster, furniture and bedspread. I pulled my feet back against the encroaching light of the fire, sure it would blacken my skin if it touched me. It continued to build, the glow turning into an inferno in seconds, the forms cast by the fire undulating together in a symphony of movement that reveled in the destruction happening so close.

Too close.

Bloody fuck — the shop.

"Erik!"

Kerry's cry ripped my attention away from the licking, hypnotic figures. I jumped out of bed and pulled on shorts. I was only seconds behind Kerry, but it felt like hours. I ran down the stairs and out of the front door, still wide open from Kerry's frantic dash, and careened around the corner of the house to find our dive shop, the dock and boats engulfed in flames.

The whine of the fire scratched at my eardrums, each pop sending painful jolts from my chest to the ends of every nerve in my toes, fingers and scalp. The heat was brutal, coming in waves off the building, an otherwise gentle ocean breeze feeding the crackling flames. Kerry stood back from the building, a cellphone at his ear, as he ran his fingers against his freshly buzzed scalp.

His expression betrayed his fear, but there was something else there as well, a look I'd never seen on his face before and never wanted to again. Before I could give it much thought, I heard the wail of sirens and turned to watch the fire trucks approach.

Kerry stepped back, closer to me, but still not at my side. Kerry ended his call and didn't look at me when he said, "Charlie's in there." His chest was bare, sweat-slicked from the heat of the fire. If he was feeling anything like me, he was torn between a desire to run into the raging fire to try to save Charlie and a deep panic that threatened to drag me under. I didn't know how to respond.

Thick, black smoke wrapped around us, acrid now at the back of my throat, where a cough started to build. There were hands on me, pulling me back from my shop, from the fire, from Charlie. From Kerry. They dragged us in separate directions, putting blankets around our shoulders, but I was already too hot. Kerry hadn't looked at me since I'd come plowing through our front door, but now he wouldn't look away.

I fought against the hands holding me and Kerry just shook his head, his demeanor so distant that for a second I was sure this would be his breaking point. Then he mouthed, "I'm okay." And it was enough to be sure my Kerry was still here. I stopped fighting and let them pull me across the street and onto the grass of our neighbor's yard.

I told them about Charlie, that the shop wasn't empty. The face of the emergency worker in front of me was impassive and clinical. He passed on the message to a firefighter, who jogged toward the building. Kerry kept watch over me, even though they continued to keep us apart. His worried eyes were on me, following each movement of the emergency worker's hands.

"Your house will be okay. They have the fire under control now," the EMS said.

I nodded. It was the least of my worries, yet I was relieved to hear it.

"Your boyfriend is okay, too."

I looked at him, searching for the judgment that usually accompanied that word. I hoped to find his concern was genuine even while the urge to defend was already

44

building in me. But all I saw in his face was understanding, the clinical coldness now evaporated.

"Thanks," I replied, tears filling my eyes.

He stood and motioned to the EMS worker next to Kerry, who leaned down and pulled the blanket from his shoulders. Kerry's eyes were feverish as he started toward me. Gone was the golden shine of his skin, replaced by a sickly orange pallor that appeared to illuminate him from the inside. He sat down heavily next to me, his knee and arm brushing against mine. I shivered despite the heat.

I was just starting to catch up to what I saw in front of me. Our shop was on the verge of collapse and the dock and boats beyond it were also in flames. Had it really only been a few hours since we'd celebrated Kerry's birthday? It felt like days, years, this moment completely disconnected from every other one in my life. Separate. Stark. Bright. Ugly. My thoughts collided with each other, filling my head with dark images that left me empty.

How had this happened?

Charlie.

My uncle. His legacy, my family.

That look in Kerry's eyes.

What about the boats. Were they okay?

Charlie.

Would we be okay? We could rebuild.

Charlie.

Every time I thought about Charlie, I flinched. I *knew* he hadn't made it out. I felt a void growing inside me. This couldn't be happening. This couldn't be real.

"You can rebuild," Kerry whispered next to me, his voice too distant.

I didn't bother to correct him—*you* instead of *we*. Even after two years as my business partner, Kerry still thought of our company as mine. The lights of the emergency vehicles—police, fire and ambulance—swirled around us, unnaturally lighting the neighborhood in pulses of red, blue and yellow. The police had arrived soon after the

45

fire trucks, but they kept away from us, as if we were as dangerous as the fire raging behind them.

Kerry's hand grazed mine. It was barely a touch, but I saw the defensive stance of the officers who watched us too closely. I glared, a challenge in my eyes, but I didn't reach to take Kerry's hand in mine. I didn't have the strength to fight this battle, not now, as the beams of the roof began to collapse and the firefighters yelled for everyone to stay clear.

I watched years of my uncle's and my life shudder then splinter into pieces. The fire slowed, starting to die under the weight of the water. The roar was gone, replaced by the whisper of flames as they licked the structure clean of all shape and form. I could hear the satisfaction of the fire as it devoured the last of our shop, sucking the final drops of marrow from the blackened bones.

I hugged my knees to my chest and rocked, struggling to understand how this had happened so fast. How it had happened at all.

Kelle raced across the lawn and threw herself into Kerry's arms. She mumbled something against his shoulder and Kerry froze for a moment then tucked his head against hers and whispered a reply into her ear.

I could only imagine what they were saying to each other. I watched them clinically, much like I imagined the EMT had assessed me earlier. Kelle's shoulders shook, her sobs ones of relief. She hugged him fiercely, and Kerry pulled her closer, taking a deep breath. When he exhaled, I blinked to clear my vision, because for a moment his breath appeared to be a stream of black smoke. They seemed to melt into each other, Kerry giving himself over to her, and I had to be losing my sanity, because I could see the moment he let down his defenses and let her give him the strength he needed. Her and not me.

The Irish twins. Finding comfort in each other.

I looked away.

"They think someone set the fire on purpose," Kelle

said. And I realized that some amount of time had passed because Kelle now sat between Kerry and me, her hand clasped protectively around his. A look passed between Kelle and Kerry that I barely noticed.

"Why would someone do that?" Everything was still too hazy.

Kelle's eyes flicked to Kerry's. "For money."

I stared at the remains of the shop and the smoldering remnants of our dock and boats and couldn't figure out why money would matter right now.

"Who would get money…?" My voice trailed off as her words clicked into place and I realized what Kelle was saying to me. "Me?" I whispered. "They think I set my shop on fire? With Charlie in it?" I was frantic, I knew, but I couldn't grasp anything besides pure, white-hot anger.

It seared through me, disbelief propelling it forwards, the rage of judgment, years of being scrutinized for what I was rather than who, blazing a path for the anger to take hold in every cell of my body. I stood, shaking, determined to make them see, to understand that I was dying inside, that this fire couldn't have come from me. I didn't know how this had happened so quickly, but it was stripping away everything I loved.

Arms were around my waist, pulling at me, urging me to sit, soothing words spilling out, and I snapped out of it because it wasn't Kerry holding me, it was Kelle. She'd never touched me, had never liked me, and yet at that moment I believed she cared, and that was all it took for me to rein myself back in.

Her arms remained wrapped around me as I gulped air. My lungs fought the burn, soot and ashes that passed over my tongue and down my throat. I coughed, tried to push her away, and yet she hung on, and I found my arms around her as she buried her face in my chest.

It took a moment for my unfocused eyes to realize what I was looking at. I thought the firefighter exiting the blackened remains of the shop was carrying a pile of blankets, and the reality came screaming at me. I inhaled sharply, rocking back as if I'd been slapped in the face. Kelle wrinkled her brow then followed my stare across the street to where the firefighter was laying the tiny bundle down on a gurney.

It was too tiny, I tried to tell myself. That couldn't be Charlie. Even if he was dead they wouldn't cover his face, I tried to rationalize, even though I knew that made no sense. Kelle burst into tears, collapsed into me, and I couldn't hold my wall up anymore. I crumpled into her and sobbed, our mourning binding us together in a way that felt backwards and wrong because these were events that never should have happened, let alone brought us closer.

I felt Kerry's arms come around us both, felt his sigh as he pulled us both into his protective embrace. Kelle and I wept openly while Kerry held us, shielding us from the prying eyes of police, firefighters and neighbors who believed I was cruel enough to kill a friend and burn my life to the ground.

"Come stay with me. You shouldn't be here," Kelle whispered into my chest.

I wanted to say yes, I didn't know if I could stay here right now, but Kerry's voice cut me off before I started speaking, his tone vicious and raw. "I won't let them drive Erik out of his home."

I couldn't understand his anger, yet it spoke to me, clearing my head. "Okay," I replied and Kelle repeated it softly.

Kerry took me in his arms that night, soothing me with his hands and his lips. We made love, slowly, softly, more gently than in any of the three years we'd been together.

I should have known then. But I didn't.

I slept.

And in the morning he was gone.

Chapter Four

I woke to the smell of smoke and burnt plastic. The scent was still fresh, like that of a bonfire recently doused. I wondered if the ashes were still hot and my stomach rolled at the thought. I turned onto my side and fought down the bile, biting into my cheek until I tasted blood.

Then I heard it.

Nothing.

I listened to the absolute silence around me, straining to hear anything besides the abyss that screamed in my ears. The space beside me was cold, long ago abandoned. I shivered.

If my Kerry were here, in our home, then he wouldn't have let me wake up alone. But the Kerry I loved had started fading away weeks ago.

I pressed the thought down, deeper than the pain of Charlie. Because even as it felt wrong to think it, I knew that Charlie's death could never hurt as much as this.

This.

There was a knock at the door. Short, hesitant, regretful. The silence of the house stretched around the wooden reverberation, muffling it.

The knock came again. And still no one answered it. Kerry wasn't here.

I knew then—the life I'd built was gone.

Everything was gone.

Because *he* was gone.

I refused to open my eyes. *This can't be real*, I chanted over and over again. The thought was becoming repetitious, meaningless. There was another knock, this time louder but still apologetic. I was naked, my body sore from Kerry's presence inside me only hours ago. I swung my legs over the edge of the bed, and stumbled when I tried to stand. I dressed, brushed my teeth, avoiding the haggard face in the mirror, and went downstairs and opened the door.

"Where is he, Kelle?"

She looked diminutive, her shoulders hunched. A silver skirt flowed around her waist and down her legs, giving her an ethereal appearance. She didn't look at me, but instead at a white envelope she held in her hands. From the unfocused glaze of her eyes, I know she didn't see that, either.

"What is it?" I reached for the envelope and she drew back with a hiss of breath.

Her eyes were red, puffy, and down her cheeks were two thick tracks where tears had recently been pouring, but her eyes were dry when she finally looked up and answered, "Just listen to Joel, yeah?"

I'd been so focused on her, I hadn't even noticed the man standing behind her. Joel was a family friend, my uncle's attorney for twenty years and mine for three. He'd watched me grow up and helped my uncle through the preparations of transferring the business to me and eventually including Kerry.

I left the door wide open and stalked toward the kitchen, anger igniting inside me. I was about to cross the threshold when I realized that was *his* favorite room and I froze.

I rotated on my heel, trying to think of some place in the house I couldn't picture him, but his presence was everywhere I looked. I squeezed my eyes shut, crossed my arms and took deep breaths. Neither Kelle nor Joel deserved me lashing out at them. My anger was reserved for one person from now on.

This couldn't be real.

But it was. And if I was going to survive it, if I wanted to survive this, then I needed to know. I opened my eyes and steeled myself, shutting off the ache in my chest, refusing to give it any kind of purchase. "Get on with it, Joel," I said through clenched teeth.

Joel and Kelle stepped inside but didn't sit. Kelle sagged against the wall and he moved to support her, but she waved him off.

He cleared his throat, "Mr Kiernan Callaghan and I have been meeting over the last couple weeks to finalize paperwork for the transfer of the business back to a sole proprietorship. All the documents are now signed, witnessed and legally filed with the appropriate agencies and localities. As of today, all the assets and liabilities of Great White Adventures are now solely yours."

I nodded. "And Mr Callaghan is...?"

"As of today, he is no longer a legal resident of South Africa."

Was I breathing?

Weeks. The word echoed in my brain, shredding my world into tiny, disconnected pieces. Kiernan had been meeting with Joel for weeks. Planning to leave me *for weeks.*

A low hum started in the back of my head and fuzzed out my hearing completely. I saw Joel's lips moving, I accepted the paperwork he handed to me, then he and Kelle left. I'd expected her to gloat, to tell me she'd been right all along. That Charlie and my mad assumptions of what Kerry wanted from life were what had driven her brother away. But she didn't. I never found out what was in the envelope in Kelle's hands. I didn't think I wanted to know.

I sat on the wood floor and opened the packet, scattering the pages in front of me. Kiernan's loopy signature stood out amongst the clear typeset on the forms, the blue ink it was written in providing irrefutable proof of those printed words and his acceptance of it all. I skimmed over the statements and clauses, my temper growing steadily out of control as I read.

Reason for dissolution of partnership—*Irreconcilable differences.*

Why hadn't I known we'd had something to reconcile?

Then, attached as an addendum to a government form, a statement from Mr Kiernan Callaghan as to the specifics of the requested dissolution — *Mr Callaghan does not wish to leave South Africa. However, there is an irreconcilable conflict between Mr Callaghan and Mr Hash on the future of Great White Adventures. Mr Callaghan enjoys his work immensely, but is unable to continue working with Mr Hash. Therefore, a formal dissolution is requested so each party may pursue their business interests individually, as they see fit.*

"Fuck you!" I screamed. I wanted to tear the house apart. How could it have only been weeks ago that I had told him his heart was never in the wrong place? I grabbed fistfuls of my hair and clamped my eyes shut, but the thoughts wouldn't stop. How could I have been so wrong? Anger surged through me and I had no one to take it out on, no one left to listen. So I did the only thing I could. I forced the pain back, pushed it down, out of my view. I fed it to the fury and hurt that simmered just below the surface, but still far enough down that I could deny it existed at all.

I waited until my hands stopped shaking. Then I stacked the papers, taking time to line up the edges. I put the paperclip back on and placed them into the envelope and looked at the clock. Twelve hours since Kiernan's party, eight hours since the fire, six since he last touched me, since I'd belonged to him completely. But now was the most important moment of my life.

Now was when I let that part of me die.

* * * *

I spent the next week in a haze. A trip to my banker confirmed the stack of legal documents. Kiernan was gone. The business was now solely mine. The banker told me I was broke, or nearly broke. Due to Kiernan's sudden disappearance, the police had enough cause to freeze my accounts pending the arson investigation. The cash I had on hand was enough for two weeks, maybe three.

I didn't understand what was happening. How had my life got to this point without any warning? The boats had been a complete loss in the fire, so Abraham canceled every charter we had scheduled, some booked two years in advance. I didn't know where Charlie's parents lived or how to get hold of them. Kiernan's paper records had been destroyed, but the police were able to track Charlie's parents down. When they refused to take custody of Charlie's body, Abraham and I bought a plot just outside town and laid him to rest.

After the funeral, we met with the deckhands and Dominick. We packed into the living room of my house and drank. Every one of them looked years older than when I'd last seen them only a week ago. From the way their eyes darted away from mine, I knew I frightened some of them now, and they weren't the only ones.

The captains of the two competing companies avoided me, as did most of the residents of Van Dyks Bay, people I'd spent my entire life around. I took it all personally, allowing their ignorance and betrayal to feed my anger.

The police would probably have avoided my calls if I'd tried to reach out to them, but I didn't. We were long past the time of statements and evidence gathering. The investigation was open and ongoing.

And Kelle? I hadn't seen or heard from her since the day she had showed up with Joel.

I avoided the water and especially the sharks. In the early hours before sunrise, I heard the tourist boats getting ready to leave, heard the clank of a cage being lifted on deck, the slap of wetsuits being piled high, of chum buckets being filled with slop. I wanted to hate the sounds, but I missed them. I missed the sharks.

I sat in Kiernan's spot on the couch, one of his novels in my hands, and stared at the door. He'd taken nothing with him and I couldn't decide whether to burn it all or leave it be as a macabre shrine to a relationship that no longer existed. I didn't drink. That would have been too cliché. I didn't melt down. I just did nothing. For hours that became days, and days that became weeks.

* * * *

Slowly, my mind began to clear and I started to consider what should happen next. I wondered if the question came down to whether I wanted to live or die. But that was too melodramatic for me to take seriously. So I decided, if it didn't matter either way, I would wait and see what happened.

Of course, that was when Kelle came knocking at my door.

"I've been offered a job as a captain." She was standing on my threshold, her hair cut short, another flowing skirt, tank top and no shoes making her look more like a pixie than the bulldog I knew her to be.

I nodded. I didn't give a shit where she ended up.

"I want you to come with me, Hash."

She stood only a few inches past the door, and it seemed like miles. There was no way I'd just heard her right. "I'm not *doff*, but I don't get it."

"I want you to come work for me."

"*Ja*, I heard you. But why?"

"Can I come in?"

I motioned her into the living room. She went for the couch, automatically going for the spot next to me, where she normally would have perched when Kerry was in his reading spot. She hesitated when she realized where she was headed and sat in the chair across from me instead.

"You look like shite."

"Cheers to you, too, Kelle belle."

She blanched but didn't take my bait. "I've hired on to a private yacht and I need an experienced person to be my co-captain. I'm looking for a dive master with extensive mechanical knowledge and the ability to pilot. I need someone who can leave in days, no strings attached." She paused. "I need someone I can trust."

"What a strange world we now live in."

"Aye. How long will it take you to be ready?"

"I have nothing, Kelleigh." I laughed darkly. "That will be easy to pack."

She nodded. "Friday then. That will give you four days to finalize what you need to. I'll book your ticket out with me."

Two days after I left South Africa, they caught the men who'd set the fire. By then, I was too far gone to care.

Chapter Five

Three years later

The ship we'd ended up on was named *Trini's Passion*, but Trini didn't care for the open ocean or sailing. She was a Fortune 500 CEO, one of the power players, and I'd seen her on the ship once in three years — when it was docked in Catalina, California. Her husband Ed, on the other hand, was a happily kept man who insisted the ship must have a female name.

Suva, the capital of Fiji, was our current stop and I'd been sent to town for provisions. My legs wobbled as I maneuvered around a tiny, ancient woman selling passionfruit out of a woven basket next to the market. Her hands were wrinkled and knotted at the joints and I couldn't turn away when she pushed the piece of fruit toward me. I knelt and took the fruit with both hands, accepting it as if it were a gift, before offering her a few coins from my pocket. She smiled, a patchwork of teeth showing behind her eager grin.

I didn't care for Suva. The port was cramped, full of tourists and beggars, and much more Westernized than I was comfortable with anymore. I preferred Nadi, across the island, but we'd only stopped in Fiji to re-provision the ship before sailing north, and traveling around to Nadi would have taken time we didn't have. The deckhands were completing minor repairs and routine maintenance while I went into town for the boss's last-minute shopping list.

The ground seemed to move underneath me when I stood

up, and I had to pause to regain my balance. In the last three years, I'd spent more time at sea than on land and I wasn't used to the dragging pull of gravity on my body. The sway of the open ocean was more familiar and infinitely more comforting.

I felt the surge of the ocean in my body as I walked, as if the land beneath me was rippling. It used to take me three days after an extended time at sea to regain my land legs, but I hadn't been on shore long enough in years to test that theory. I didn't enjoy being in the city and I found myself moving faster to finish my shopping list and return to the ship.

I felt trapped on land, limited, frustrated by the ability to only move forwards or back. In the ocean, none of those limitations existed.

A man pushing a cart jostled me from behind, and I had to fight to regain my balance to avoid tripping into the growing sea of people around me. The market was packed and each step I took deeper into the crowd ratcheted my frustration up one more level. At one time I'd been a people person, some might have even called me charming, but now I dreaded the push of human beings around me, all of us breathing the same air. It was stifling.

Even among the Indian and dark Fijian native faces surrounding me, there were enough tourists present for me to easily mix with the crowd that browsed the market stalls. My blond hair had grown long enough for me to pull it into a ponytail that my crew loved to tease me endlessly about it, calling me the pirate of *Trini's Passion*, the sixty-meter ship on which I worked as co-captain and dive master.

When I spoke, which was as little as possible, whether on land or at sea, my South African accent was usually confused for British or Aussie. I rarely corrected the inaccuracy.

In other places, my height alone, just under two meters, drew attention, but in places like Suva that catered to the Western traveler, I was one of a handful of tall men within sight. I smiled politely when the women in the market tried to reel me in with their feminine charms, inviting me to learn more about them and their wares.

I paid for a gallon-size bottle of Bounty Rum, shuddering as I picked it up and dropped it into my shopping bags. I didn't know how my boss, Ed, was able to drink that shit. It was the last item on my list. It was as I was headed toward the harbor where we were docked that I heard it. The voice I'd been traveling the world to forget.

A few steps in front of me, a black-haired man with a hint of golden tan chuckled heartily with the Indian man next to him. They walked along companionably, their smiles and demeanor easy and languid.

I stopped in my tracks. Kiernan hadn't seen me yet. I fisted my hands in the straps of the bags I carried, using the weight of them to balance me, to keep me on my feet, as I tried to rein in the anger already flooding my veins. Below me, the ground shifted again, and I struggled to find my equilibrium.

All around me, the colors, sounds and smells of the market became overwhelming and garish, too foreign, because that laugh cutting through me was too familiar, like home.

He was beautiful. I knew that it shouldn't have mattered that he hadn't changed, but it did, and my temper flared to think that he could still have any man he wanted. And he didn't want me.

The two men were so engrossed in their conversation, it wasn't until Kiernan had to sidestep around me that he actually saw me. The recognition was instant but fleeting. He lowered his eyes, and I couldn't decipher the expression on his face — frustration? — but his speech never faltered and his steps never slowed. There was little in his demeanor to suggest he saw me as anything more than an obstacle in his path. Ignoring me in public was second nature to him.

Some things never changed.

My heart beat erratically in my chest as his gaze slid coolly away from mine and he walked deeper into the market. I stumbled on, refusing to look back, determined to be as unaffected by his sudden appearance as he had been by mine.

But I couldn't do it. My hands shook, the bottles of liquor clacked loudly together and I wondered if I would be able to make it to the ship without them shattering. Tears stung the edges of my eyes, but I wouldn't let them fall. Not for him. Not again.

* * * *

I staggered onto the ship, dropping the bags at the stairs leading down to the galley.

"Mr Hash, are you okay?" Mela asked, the familiarity of her clipped South African accent unexpectedly soothing.

"*Lekker*," I responded, letting the Afrikaans slang slip through as I tried to force a smile to convince her. "Could you take these down to the galley, please?"

She nodded and I took the stairs up to the bridge two at a time.

I pushed through the glass doors and ignored the petite brunette at the helm as I booted up my workstation. My hands were shaking and I had to enter my password three times before I got it right. I swore under my breath and Kelle shot me an annoyed look that immediately turned to sympathy when she really looked at me.

"You saw him. Bloody fuck." She ran her fingers through her chestnut hair, cut in an angular pixie that flattered her high cheekbones. Her face was drawn and her emotions more restrained than I would have expected under the circumstances. Her Irish accent sounded thicker. "I didn't know he was going to be here. Wouldn't have stopped at this port if I had."

I narrowed my eyes and studied her. She had obviously run into him earlier when she'd gone on shore for the boss, but hadn't said anything to me before I set out. Kelle was a tough captain, but never manipulative, and our relationship had been purely professional for years. She'd probably decided against warning me, thinking I would resent her butting in. She was right.

"I know," I responded, turning back to the computer.

I flipped through the logbook files, checking the status of repairs to be completed before we put out for Borneo. Kelle didn't push the subject. She worked with the GPS and weather forecast system, plotting the route that would take us about seven days to complete. She worked silently, her brows furrowed in concentration. She really was a lovely woman. I stole glances of her as we worked side by side and for the thousandth time, I thanked God that she didn't look anything like her brother. I typed a couple of notations and closed the maintenance file to head off the bridge and check in with the crew.

Before the glass door shut behind me, Kelle's voice stopped me cold. "Kiernan had his reasons for leaving, Erik."

Her casual use of my first name, for the first time in years, was enough to send me through the roof. Only Kiernan had ever called me that. I turned and saw her face coldly reflecting her dismissive tone.

Her attempt to casually explain away Kiernan's betrayal made me flinch. The meaning behind her words couldn't have been more damning and hurtful.

"Fuck you, Kelle. I don't give a shit what his reasons were. You saw the paperwork. He thought we had an 'irreconcilable conflict' about the operation of the company. Maybe if I'd left the Cape, and signed the business over to him, he would've stayed."

"You're wrong. 'Twas never about the business. It's hard enough being an out gay man now, let alone in South Africa or anywhere on the Dark Continent. Executing gays is still legal in some parts of Africa. Just because you haven't ever given a shit about your own survival, about whether you live or die today, doesn't mean it was easy for Kiernan to say fuck it all and stick around. You didn't give him a choice."

"A choice!" I yelled, my temper now past explosive. "I offered him the world. I asked him to fucking marry me and he ran."

"That's not fair and you know it."

I laughed, not seeing any humor in this situation, or that it had taken three years for us to finally have this out. "Not fair. Right. Kiernan disappears in the middle of the night after our shop burns down and you're telling me I'm not being fair?"

"He was scared!"

"You know what? Fuck you both. I'm done talking about this. *I* was scared by the fire. And when I turned to my partner, the man I loved, the man I trusted with my life, he was gone. All traces of him wiped away, because he'd been planning his exit for weeks. He didn't leave because he was scared, he left because I was in his way. Kiernan doesn't deserve your excuses. And don't you even think of trying to get a message to him. If he sets foot on this boat, I'm gone."

* * * *

I stormed down to my cabin and slammed the door. A part of me knew I was taking old anger out on the wrong person, because Kiernan had abandoned his sister as easily as he had me. He'd abandoned everyone, friends and family, cutting ties with us all when he left South Africa. So why she was trying to defend him now only confused me.

For three years Kelle and I had been able to work together without one word about Kiernan or why he'd done what he had. Three years for my anger to fester, the hurt never lessening, and it had only taken five seconds in a market to leave me feeling trapped, rooted to the ground, unable to escape the pulse of people around me. I needed to get back out to sea.

While I had grown up on the water, dedicated my life and my livelihood to it many years ago, it was only recently that

I'd begun to grasp how much I needed it. I tried not to think that I'd only traded one addiction for another — Kiernan for the ocean.

I paced my tiny room, caught between frustration, anger and sadness. I couldn't stand still, and being docked aggravated the sense of claustrophobia creeping in on me since the market. The clock on my nightstand showed we had only hours left in port, and with all the maintenance almost completed, I'd have little to do until we set out to sea.

A loud knock on my cabin door jangled my nerves until I heard Mela's voice on the other side. "I brewed *rooibos*, Mr Hash."

I stopped pacing. I couldn't have requested anything more perfect. I opened the door and pulled her into a bear hug. I was sure she'd heard the exchange between Kelle and I, everyone on the ship had to have, and somehow she'd known exactly what I needed when I had no idea.

"Is Ed on board?" I asked when I reluctantly let her go.

"No, he took off again. And I'm headed out, too, with Georges and Samuel."

Great, I'd managed to scare them all away. I shook my head. "I'm sorry, Mela."

She grasped my hands. "Go get some tea, yeah?"

I kissed her forehead and walked to the galley, where I could smell the sweet earthiness of *rooibos* tea wafting from the pot on the stove. Although I was already regretting the outburst with Kelle, I was grateful for the time alone. I needed it to calm down.

I spooned sugar into my *rooibos* tea as I poured the cream. The clink of the spoon on the side of the cup sounded hollow, and I knew I looked like a *doff* trying to find his future in the swirl of the orange-red liquid. I'd not thought about Kiernan in months. Definitely the longest span of time since he'd abandoned our business and me and I'd sought shelter on *Trini's Passion*.

I was thrown by how much seeing him had stung. But

I shouldn't have been surprised. The insurance company had yet to settle on my fire claim and the criminal case had closed only days ago. How could I possibly put that part of my life behind me when it had never ended? But I was surprised at how angry I still was. My temper usually came in blasts and then all was forgiven and I moved on, no grudges. Except when it came to Kiernan.

I couldn't deny that seeing him had dredged up more than just anger and pain. A part of me had leaped when I'd seen the smile on his face. Kiernan's lips were thick, pouty even, and I had loved lavishing attention on them. They were like magnets for me and Kiernan had teased me that I went teenage schoolgirl whenever he licked his lips. Even now, the memories of the wicked things Kiernan had done with those lips had me shifting in my seat.

"Trini tells me this may be your last trip with us," my boss said as he took a seat across from me in the galley, coffee cup in hand. His sudden appearance made me jump and I couldn't hold back the blush from what I'd been thinking of when he walked in, but as usual, Ed was unaware.

I struggled to remember what Ed had just asked me and then realized Trini must have filled him in on the outcome of the trial. "It's possible."

"That case of yours finally got settled?"

"Something like that." I was hesitant to share any details with the boss, personal or non-personal. This one happened to be really personal and I wished Trini hadn't said anything to her ditzy husband. In the end, my possible departure would affect him more than her, but she was still my employer.

"Trini won't be able to meet us in Borneo."

I sat back, twirling the tea in my cup. "*Isit?* Are we still making our way there then?" I already knew the answer to my question, but when the boss was in a talking mood I had to listen.

"She said to go and enjoy myself. So why not?" He sipped his coffee, his bright pink shirt half unbuttoned, revealing a mass of brown chest hair. I couldn't help thinking, maybe if he cleaned up a bit, Trini might want him around more. He was a sturdy man, stereotypical American in many ways, the same height as me, with thinning curly brown hair, warm brown eyes, a George Hamilton tan and parrothead wardrobe. He was a token husband, an ex-baseball player well past his prime, and he was a chop if I ever met one, but always kind. Ed's next words broke me out of my reverie.

"We're taking on a couple extra hands. I have guests flying in to meet us in Phuket for diving in two weeks."

Despite the incessant Fijian heat, my veins turned to ice. How hadn't I seen this coming?

Of course Kelle would pick today to push me on Kiernan's vanishing act. She knew Ed was looking for more crew and her brother would be at the top of the recommended list. He was a certified dive master with a UK passport, not to mention pleasant to look at, which seemed to trump all other qualifications when Ed had guests to impress.

I tried to keep my voice calm and not choke on the *rooibos* that singed my throat as I swallowed the urge to scream. My next words came out more strangled than I wanted them to sound.

"You have anybody in mind?"

"Not yet," he answered, and I relaxed. I still had time to make sure I wasn't trapped on this ship with him. My gut feeling was, despite her earlier defense of him, Kelle wanted Kiernan on this ship as little as I did. "There's no need to hurry on to Borneo since Trini won't be meeting us, so I'm thinking we'll spend a day or two in port, pick up a few hands and then head out to sea."

"Kelle and I will hit the bars tonight and talk to our contacts." *Because there is no way in hell I'm letting you make this decision*, I thought.

"Great. You know what I'm looking for. "

I resisted the urge to roll my eyes. "Yes, sir."

Chapter Six

We were only days away from the December solstice and the days continued to lengthen. The sun hovered above the horizon, rings of bright red and orange reflecting off the wispy clouds floating over the harbor. I found Kelle on the bridge, not long after Ed had taken off again in search of sparkly things to distract him for the night. As soon as I walked in, she said, "I don't want him here any more than you do."

That was all I needed to hear.

Immediately, I felt as if we were on to something more, a different relationship than either of us had tried in the six years we'd known each other. With one short and explosive conversation, we'd broken through a barrier. We were now united in the singular goal of keeping Kiernan off *Trini's Passion*.

Once we'd decided to start our scouting trip, she took her usual five minutes to get ready while I labored in front of the closet trying to figure out what to wear. I finally settled on a blue T-shirt and green cargo shorts, mostly because they were the last two clean items of clothing I had until Mela finished the laundry. I tried to tell myself it wasn't because Kiernan had always loved me in blue, but I wasn't fooling myself or Kelle. She just shook her head when I met her on deck.

"I was really hoping to make it home for Christmas." Kelle shrugged her shoulders, put on her sunglasses and allowed me to help her off the gangplank and onto the dock. She wore a white tank top, long hippie skirt and flip-flops. Ever the pixie, with her high cheekbones, thin frame and graceful movements, she looked like anything but the captain of a luxury yacht, and a brilliant one at that.

I glanced at Kelle as we walked. She appeared completely relaxed, despite Ed's idiocy and the sudden appearance of her estranged brother. She'd refined her ability to keep her cool and I envied her as I tended to wear my heart on my sleeve. She was also decisive, head-spinningly so sometimes, which was in direct contrast to my tendency to endlessly explore options, but that was why we made a good team.

We walked into downtown Suva, side by side, an uneasy, but not unpleasant, quiet between us.

"I know your parents would've liked to see you for the holiday." With Ed's new plans, we would either be off the coast of Borneo or in Thailand for Christmas, leaving both of us on the job until he and his guests decided to head home or on to another destination. We could be on this leg of the trip longer than either of us knew, but that was the life we'd chosen.

Kelle shrugged and echoed my thoughts, "I know what I signed up for. Ma and Da'll understand."

"So where we going first? Traps or O'Reilly's?"

"He'll be at O'Reilly's."

"Traps it is. You know, Kelle. I don't want to damage this, well, whatever this…not hating each other thing is…"

Kelle had just as little patience as I did. "Just speak, Hash."

I stopped outside the door to Traps and tentatively put my hand on her arm. "I feel like I'm missing something. Why don't you want Kiernan on your ship?"

She looked so sad, I was sorry I'd asked. "I just assumed you knew."

I shook my head.

"When Kiernan left, he cleared out our shared account. Took everything. I signed on to this gig with Trini because I was broke. Nothing left. Couldn't even make it back to Belfast if I'd wanted to."

I pulled her into a quick hug.

"I'm sorry," I whispered.

She leaned into my chest and we held each other for a moment. It was the most physical contact we'd had since the night Charlie died, and I couldn't remember if it had been me or her who had first set up those boundaries between us. I was happy to see them fading.

She patted my back and pulled away, a shy smile on her lips. "Thanks, Hash."

I opened the door for her, the sound of Jack Johnson floating above the voices and laughter inside, and was pounced on almost immediately.

A gigantic man pulled us into a bear hug, enveloping us both beneath the ropes of his arms.

"Good to see you, Moose," I said once he released us both from his grip.

He pulled out a stool at the bar for Kelle and brought over two beers. "I heard you were in town, but I thought it was only for the day."

"Was only to be one day. We're delayed. Need to pick up a couple hands. Our itinerary changed," Kelle answered and took a long drink from her beer.

"Whatcha looking for?"

"Master divers, if you know any looking for a three- to four-week assignment. No American passports, please. And you know Ed. He will want someone who is…visually appealing." She snickered.

Moose rolled his eyes, but I recognized the glint of mischief from years of being on the receiving end of it.

"Don't even think about it, fucker," I immediately responded. "We're not interested in taking him on, so tell us who else you got."

"Things still that strained?"

"Not your business, yeah?"

Moose laughed heartily. "Fair enough. Yes, I have a married couple I can recommend. Both dive masters. She can bartend, he can do mechanical. They're about as pretty as they come. I think they'd be open to a short assignment.

Hang out here long enough and they'll be by. I'll introduce you."

"Thanks, Moose." Kelle lifted herself off the bar stool and pulled Moose down to kiss him on the forehead.

An hour later, we were well on our way to being shit-faced. Moose, Kelle and I held court at a table near the front where a steady stream of water-based crew, people who had passed in and out of our lives through the years, stopped by to say hello and share a drink.

It had been a long time since I'd last done a bar night like this, and I'd forgotten how small the ship community was, especially considering how big the oceans were and how many miles of coast circled the globe. Ours was a world of three degrees of separation instead of six.

The crew we didn't know would pull up a chair and we'd discover where we were connected. A place, a name, a skill that set you apart. Deals were made at the table. Crews brought on, hands trading gigs for the ship or destination they wanted, people slipping away two by two, or sometimes in groups, to fill the emptiness that was unavoidable if you spent any time at sea. It was the way our community worked—handshakes in smoky bars, hurried blow jobs in bathrooms, pints of ale lubricating the mind, making you feel like maybe living at sea for months or years at a time wasn't as unnatural as you thought, convincing you that everything would be better in the world if humans could just free themselves from the land.

We talked music, politics, sports, stories from whatever country we each called home, either for the night or from long ago. Moose's married couple showed up during a particularly heated debate on football and bought Kelle and I another round and we drank it, really enjoying each other's company for the first time ever, as we debriefed them on the nuances of our ship. Moose was right, they were perfect for the job and beautiful to boot.

Kelle and I exchanged glances, grateful the recruitment had been this easy.

More pints were passed and snippets of the night began to float by unconnected. More conversation, more laughter, more music, dancing and shots of Fijian rum that, even in my drunkenness, still made me shudder from the turpentine taste.

Kelle disappeared, then reappeared, and she and Moose were dragging me somewhere because I'd forgotten how to make my legs work on land.

Then someone's tongue was in my mouth, and it could have been Moose, it could have been someone else, I hoped it wasn't Kiernan. At the same time, I wondered if he would still taste the same.

But it didn't matter who it was tonight, because I needed to be lost, to be buried under gallons of ale and rum, sheathed tightly into anyone that could make me forget that gaping emptiness. Because Kelle was right, I didn't care if I died. And if I woke up tomorrow morning deathly thirsty, head pounding, but sated, with one less night taken over by the unrelenting acrid smoke I couldn't wipe from my memory or my dreams, then the risk was worth it.

And if for some reason I didn't wake up, that was okay, too.

* * * *

Consciousness came back to me the same way it had been lost last night, piece by piece. I heard muffled whispers first, the scratch of a coffee cup on a wooden table, realized there was light behind my closed eyes and felt movement on the bed next to me as a warm leg brushed mine. My stomach rolled but didn't threaten, and the cool breeze drifting over my naked skin in waves from the ceiling fan above helped clear the fuzziness in my brain.

"...don't know if the insurance company has settled yet. The trial just finished."

It was Kelle's voice, which meant I was in Moose's bed and she was most likely sitting at his kitchen table, only steps away in the cramped studio apartment. It wasn't the first time either of us had ended up back at Moose's apartment in the city, but the first time we'd woken up here together. I groaned and curled into a ball against the body at my side, burying my face into the enormous man's back.

"Good morning, sunshine," Moose whispered, always predictable, a low chuckle rumbling through his chest and reverberating like tiny daggers through my head.

"Sssssshhhh," I chastised him, moving closer to his warm skin.

Moose and Kelle continued to talk as I faded in and out of awareness. They were discussing me, my nightmare with the insurance company, the trial and police. The surreal nightmare I was beginning to think really would become never-ending, but I couldn't muster the energy to contribute anything to their discussion.

It was only when Moose squeezed my hip one more time before rolling out of bed, taking his warmth with him, that I reluctantly opened my eyes. The sound of bacon frying and the heavenly scent of coffee convinced me to sit up and find my clothes.

I pulled my shorts on and searched around the bed for my shirt. I was half-hidden by the screen that divided the bed from the larger room, but it offered nothing in the way of privacy from the sounds that echoed off the concrete block walls. I cringed, thinking about the show Kelle had probably been exposed to last night when she passed out on the couch. But she was all smiles this morning, looking as if she'd had nothing to drink the night before.

She pushed two aspirin and a cup of coffee at me when I sat down at the table, a questioning look on her face. "Care to weigh in on our discussion?"

I chased the aspirin with the scalding coffee, draining the cup and motioning for Moose to refill it from the pot on the stove. "Now that the criminal case is finished I expect to receive notice on the settlement. At least, that's what they told me would happen. It is still a South African business."

"Owned by an English company," Moose interjected.

"Doesn't matter," Kelle and I said almost simultaneously.

The truth was, I didn't know if I cared any more about the money. The shitheads who'd murdered Charlie, burned the shop, dock and boats were in jail, and for a really long time, from what I'd heard. It didn't bring back the shop or Charlie. Charlie's death alone should have been enough to put the men away years earlier, but the police had dragged their feet as soon as they had begun to hear the whispers about Kiernan, me and the barely legal teenager we had taken in when no one else would. Then Kiernan had disappeared and everything about their crime became about me and my perverted lifestyle.

Don't get me wrong. I loved South Africa. It was home in ways that the ocean would never be. And I was proud of the steps we as a country had taken before most of the Western world, not just Africa. Same-sex partnerships were legal, had been for years now, and discrimination was banned.

But as Africans, we struggled with tradition, or the old ways, whatever you wanted to call the ancient superstitions that refused to be relinquished even when in direct conflict to science. That, in combination with the hatred that lingered below the surface from the years of apartheid, had been enough to fuel three young men to brazenly destroy everything I'd spent my life building.

Moose dropped plates of eggs and bacon in front of us. I tried not to moan in delight at the rich taste of the bacon fat. Ed refused to keep anything so blatantly unhealthy on board. It had been too long, but Kelle beat me to it.

"Oh God, Moose. I will put up with noisy sex any night if I get to wake up to this."

I blushed furiously. "Fuck me," I said, completely flustered.

"I think Moose already did a pretty good job of that last night," Kelle replied dryly.

I'd walked right into that one. Moose laughed so hard the chair strained beneath him as he shook uncontrollably.

Kelle snickered, her lips curled at the corners, as she chewed on a bacon strip. The blush crawled up my face. I had to be just as red as last night's sunset.

Kelle was merciful. She slid her chair back and started gathering her stuff. "That couple is meeting us at the boat at eleven. We should get going soon."

I shoveled the last forkful of eggs into my mouth and leaned over to kiss Moose. He pulled me into a hug that enveloped me in his large arms and whispered in my ear, "Glad to see you and Kelle talking."

I nodded against his chest. "Thanks for last night. And breakfast," I mumbled, my words smashed together against his muscled chest.

"I'll keep an eye on Kiernan for you," Moose blurted out as we headed for the door.

Kelle and I stared at each other. I was surprised to find the expression on her face matched mine — relief. Neither of us wanted to see harm come to him. I nodded again and we left Moose happily digging into his plate of eggs and bacon.

72

Chapter Seven

Suva came to life slowly, much slower than cities in more Westernized parts of the world. It was almost nine a.m. and vendors were still setting up their shops in the market. I stopped and picked up passionfruit and bunches of cauliflower for Mela.

We discussed the next part of our trip as we walked down the main street back to port. Kelle was debating sailing north of Papua New Guinea versus south through Torres Straight when I blurted out the question I'd wanted to ask her for six years. "What's your problem with me?"

To Kelle's credit, my abruptness didn't seem to throw her nearly as much as it had me when it had escaped my lips. She sighed and kept on walking. "What can I say besides I didn't like you? It was that simple. You're too much like me, Hash. Don't look so shocked. You really think about it, you'll see it's true. I didn't have the patience to spend time figuring out how to get along with you. Sound familiar? Then when Kiernan left, I couldn't pretend there wasn't already a connection between us. I didn't know how to be friends with you, but I couldn't let you go either. I knew you still loved him as much as I did, and you hated him as much as I did. Plus, I knew I needed you on my ship. You work hard, you're smart, you know how to run a business, how to lead."

"I've always wanted to like you," I confessed.

She grabbed my hand. "I know. I'm sorry. I've approached our…relationship with more selfishness than you deserved. I was jealous. Jealous of what you had with Kerry. He chose to do things with you that he would have never done otherwise, things I couldn't convince him of. I seethed with jealousy that you could so easily become everything to him when I'd always been the one he relied on. I know it's not what you want to hear."

"No, it's not."

"It's the truth. And that feels more important."

"And now?"

She looked up at me, but I refused to meet her eyes. "What? Do I like you now?" She laughed. "Give it some time. I'm not as opposed to the idea anymore."

I resisted the urge to hug her again, knowing I was probably pushing her comfort level and not wanting to spoil our new truce. "I think we should head north," I said, bringing the conversation around to the business of the ship.

"That was my original plotting..."

Kelle's voice faded as my heart began to thunder in my ears. She was still talking, but I couldn't hear anything as the pounding in my chest pushed out all other sound and the sudden drop of my stomach made me stumble on my feet. I could see *Trini's Passion* from where we stood, but that unmistakable mass of black hair and golden skin casually leaning against the railing of the deck didn't belong there. Kiernan smiled, jarringly alive and electric. His eyes were hidden behind sunglasses but I knew exactly their shade of green and where the edges spliced off into a rough band of chocolate brown that circled the iris.

He was focused on Ed, who was waving his arms wildly, the drink in his hand splattering large red droplets down the front of his floral print shirt. They laughed loudly as Ed ended his story and Kelle's head snapped up. As soon as I heard her swear, I knew I wasn't hallucinating. Kiernan wasn't just visiting. I had the sinking feeling he was the newest member of our crew.

* * * *

I was seven the first time I went down in a shark cage. I had finally proved to my father I could hold my breath long enough to not need a regulator and I was a stronger swimmer than any of the fishermen he took out on his boat.

Uncle Ron had taken me out on the boat since I was four, when I learnt to hold my breath underwater, but my dad was his best friend and I wasn't going anywhere without Dad's approval, no matter if Uncle Ron thought I was ready or not.

But on my seventh birthday, my dad woke me up hours before dawn, a drysuit and mask in hand, and told me to get dressed. Uncle Ron was taking me to swim with the great whites.

I sat in the bow of his boat, my knees pulled into my chest and under a thick wool sweater for warmth. I knew my uncle was watching me. I could feel his gaze on me as the boat cut through the glassy water of Van Dyks Bay. In fact, the whole crew was staring at me with an expectation I didn't understand, as if they were waiting for something amazing to happen and somehow I was going to be the one to pull it off. Seal pups called loudly from the shore of Dyer Island as we anchored off its rocky shore. It was too early in the season for any pups to be born yet, but there was something unusual about the water this year, I heard my uncle say. The crew swung the cage out over the sea, fastening it to the helm of the boat, then pulled out the chum bucket. The boat rolled lazily in the currents off the island, the hills of the mainland golden tipped by the rising sun.

I don't know if I wasn't old enough to know real fear, or if even then I'd put more value on experience than my own life, but either way, my first glimpse of a four-meter great white sliding through the water, trailing after a fish head skewered on a gigantic hook, was my first real bonding experience with the water I had lived next to all my life. I ran along the sides of the boat, tracking the shark from bow to stern, mesmerized by the unhurried, powerful swish of its tail and the way its mouth hung open, showing lines of jagged teeth.

I climbed into the cage, and one of my uncle's crew members settled in next to me. We waited for the shark to circle the boat. Our heads bobbed above the water, ready to submerge when the shark reappeared.

"Left!" a deckhand yelled, signaling us to pull ourselves under the water and into the cage as the shark approached. I searched the cloudy water, saw movement, then it was just there, like a specter finding physical form.

Solid, indestructible, a sense of age that had nothing to do with the number of years it had been on this earth. A being of immutable power and immoveable solitude. Its black eyes were blank, unmoving, and I knew I should be intimidated that this creature was capable of killing me in one swift strike, but I couldn't be afraid because it didn't even register my presence.

There was blood in the water and it wasn't mine.

Only later would I learn that that was the moment my uncle knew I would take over his business. He was a superstitious man and I had passed the test.

"It's not the shark or the ocean that is the measure of a man. It is the way he reacts in the cage," my uncle would cryptically answer when I asked how it was he understood people so well.

After years aboard that boat, watching the business change from marine research to tourist charters, and the clientele from scientists to families on holiday, I felt as if I was getting closer to knowing what he meant.

Then Kiernan walked onto my boat.

As confident as I'd been my first time in the cage, Kiernan was the opposite. Kelle had nearly dragged him on board that summer day. We sighted the first great white silently cutting through the water and, after pointing out the supposed gash he'd received on his hand the night before, Kiernan refused to get into the cage. No matter what the crew or I told him about the safety of the cage or how harmless the sharks really were, he couldn't be swayed.

Then Kelle had emerged from the cage, her skin flushed from the cold water, her eyes feverish with a look of awe I knew so well, and she'd whispered something to him that made him laugh — the first time I heard that rumbling laugh that made me sway on my feet even as the boat beneath me remained steady — and he'd given in, his fingers intertwined with hers, his steps no longer hesitant.

He spent an hour in the cage, much longer than I'd expected him to last, and when he emerged, his long body sliding effortlessly out of the water, I believed we had another convert. It was only later that day, sitting at the bar with Kelle, Kiernan and my crew, that Kiernan said it was an experience he didn't ever want to repeat.

"I just don't trust they won't hurt me."

"Don't be ridiculous. Sharks rarely attack, the great whites even less so. Unless you're a seal, of course."

He dipped his head and laughed, leaning into me, and whispered a confession only I could hear. "They're so otherworldly."

It was apparent from his tone that idea frightened him, but it was exactly what I found so intriguing about the sharks, and at the same time, about the man sitting next to me at the bar. I felt a rush of heat as his leg brushed against mine and I found myself answering more honestly than I'd intended, knowing that I was replying to more than just my thoughts on the sharks. "That's what makes them beautiful."

Kiernan scoffed. "No, that's what makes them dangerous. It's a lure. They're only out for one thing." Then he'd smiled at me, eyes shining mischievously even in the low light of the bar. I'd never wanted anyone that badly.

I should have known then how dangerous he would be.

* * * *

The images of those first dives — Kiernan's and mine — battled with each other in my head as I stepped onto the

77

deck of *Trini's Passion*. Kiernan removed his sunglasses and caught me in a cool gaze that made his eyes look black. Otherworldly. Aged more than the three years we'd been apart.

Ed blithered on, unaware of the tension building on deck, "Kelle, Hash. Meet our new crew members. Kerry and Abhi have agreed to join us for the trip to Thailand." The Indian man whom I'd seen with Kiernan yesterday emerged from the main cabin, two drinks in hand, and tipped his head at us. Neither Kelle nor I spoke and Ed continued on, completely oblivious. "I met them at O'Reilly's last night. Apparently, Kiernan here is a dive master. Also from Ireland, Kelle. Perhaps the two of you can share some stories."

"Perhaps," she answered but didn't say anything further. Her voice remained strong and the coldness in her demeanor matched her twin's. She reached for my hand and pulled me away to the stairs leading to the bridge.

I could hear Ed chatting happily below, but when I looked out of the window, Kiernan was no longer watching his new employer. He hid behind his sunglasses and stared back at me, his face completely unreadable. If his nonchalance during our arrival was anything to go by, he'd known he was walking onto a ship piloted by his estranged sister and his ex-partner.

He hadn't spoken to Kelle in three years, and he'd vanished rather than spend one more moment with me. What was he thinking? Kelle was already on her cell to the married couple, apologizing profusely, but like any other person willing to pick up and leave at a moment's notice, they were as okay with staying where they were a bit longer as they would have been to travel with us. She promised to keep their contact information and signed off.

"What the fuck are we going to do about this, Hash?" The strain in her voice was evident, more so than I was sure she wanted to convey.

Through the window of the bridge, Kiernan and I were still locked in a staredown that would have been comical if I hadn't had the gut instinct this was setting up our boundaries.

I tried to convince myself I didn't have anything to lose. He was the one who'd left. He was the one who'd walked away from his sister and me when we needed him the most. Kelle and I already owned our places on this ship and he couldn't take that away from us. As idiotic as I felt thinking it, this was my territory and he would respect that.

But in reality, whatever strength I felt was a shield made of aluminum foil, shiny but ready to crumple at the first challenge.

Luckily, Ed pulled at Kiernan's arm, demanding his attention, and Kiernan broke his gaze away from mine.

Only then did I respond to Kelle's question. "Nothing. He doesn't deserve our time. We do our jobs and move on. What he does is of no consequence to us."

Kelle stood at my shoulder and I could feel more than see the moment she was with me on this. "All right. Let's finalize the route and lock it into the GPS."

* * * *

We were at sea two days before there was an opportunity for Kiernan and me to do more than cross paths. Ed suddenly decided he wanted to make a quick stop at Vanuatu for an afternoon of diving, so while Abhi suited up with Ed, Kiernan and I went down to the storage room to bring their equipment on deck. Ed still had no idea of the mess he'd brought on board, and I wanted to leave it like that. I was determined for Ed to never know and there was no reason these next three weeks couldn't be completely uneventful.

"You look good," Kiernan said to me as I bent over the tanks, testing the valves.

Of course the fuckhead had impeccable timing, waiting until I was ass in the air to throw me a compliment. I bit back any response, grinding my teeth in frustration.

He took one step closer and I tensed. "I mean it. It's...nice to see you again."

I ignored him. We worked silently, but it was as if I could see the wheels turning in his head, which was far too familiar to me even after all this time. "When we're done here, how about I make you lunch?"

"What? Fuck off!" was out of my mouth before I stopped to think.

He looked as if he was going to take a step back then stopped and crossed his arms, holding his ground, only a meter away from me. For a second, I could've sworn he smiled, but it was gone as soon as I turned around.

I continued putting Ed and Abhi's gear together and said casually, "Why the sudden mood change, Jekyll? You seemed pretty pissed at me up until now."

He flinched and struggled for words, which made me inwardly gloat a bit, so I wasn't ready for his reply.

"I was surprised to see you. Didn't expect to ever run into you in Fiji. But I can't just accept this is coincidence." He moved closer, and I could feel the heat of his body just a step away from mine, but he didn't touch me. "I'm tired of running, Erik. I can't run away from you anymore."

I realized I was holding the valve to the tank so tightly the metal strained under my fist. "We don't have time for this. Just do your job and get the hell off my ship." I heaved the tank over my shoulder along with the gear for Ed and walked out, leaving Kiernan silent in my wake.

* * * *

"What did he say to you?" Kelle asked.

I'd gone straight from the equipment hold, dropped off Ed's gear, and sprinted up to the bridge to escape. On the deck, Kiernan helped Ed into his gear. There were clouds on the horizon, but nothing that looked threatening enough to call off their dive. Kiernan wore his swim trunks hung low on his hips. I watched him move, remembering what the muscles of his lithe swimmer's body looked like when he didn't have a T-shirt on. His suit was just snug enough I didn't have to imagine how his perfectly round ass sat on those powerfully strong legs.

I blinked, cleared my throat and tried to remember what Kelle had just asked. I blushed when I realized the answer was something along the lines of what I'd just been thinking about Kiernan. "That my ass looked grand."

"Bollocks. He did not."

"He did. Not in so many words, but he did."

She tipped back in her chair and laughed. The sound echoed around the wheelhouse, eroding the tension, taking another notch off the distance between us. "What an arse." She laughed until she had to swipe tears off her cheeks. Her eyes were bright, completely open to me. There had always been an edge in our relationship, even in the last few days as those barriers began to break down, and now? It had evaporated. I smiled.

"Then he offered to make me lunch."

"And you told him to fuck off."

I gave her a look that said *How did you know?* then remembered her insistence that we had a lot in common. "He caught me off guard."

Kelle rolled her eyes. "You would've done the same thing even if you'd been prepared. Get real. He's not daft. He knows you're pissed off. Shit, everyone on this boat knows you're pissed off."

Ed and Abhi had dropped into the ocean and Kiernan sat on the deck, his back to the bridge.

"I think you forget how young he is, Hash. He was nineteen when we first met you. I was just about to turn twenty. He's only twenty-five now. You've always seen him as older than he actually is, physically and mentally. Kiernan is not an old soul, definitely not wise beyond his years. He is restrained, careful, methodical and logical, often unemotional, but you canna confuse any of those things for wisdom or maturity.

"I know that sounds horrible, but it's the truth. Kiernan

is brilliant, calm, forgiving, patient, steady, but so inwardly focused that he's never been able to really get out of his own head. He sees the world around him through a lens that confounds me. Do you know what I mean?" She tapped her fingers on the desk. Her brown eyes searched mine, trying to decide if what she was saying was getting through to me. I'm sure my face betrayed how lost I still was, and she sighed. "I've said it before. You and I are much more alike than I've been comfortable with. It's taken me this long to really understand Kiernan, and he's my brother. I canna expect you to do it at all when you're hurting this much, but I know you'll get there. And maybe that will mean you forgive him, I don't know. Maybe you'll only be able to listen and move on. There's no harm done in forgiveness. Not true forgiveness. I'm not selling you on this, am I?"

I laughed. "No."

"I'm going to tell you something I swore I never would. But you need to keep your massive temper under control and let me finish before you storm off." She waited for me to nod my assent. "I saw Kiernan the night he left South Africa."

"Fuck, Kelle!" The words were out before I could think. I balled my fists and began to pace. She waited while I fumed, taking deep breaths to calm myself.

Kelle continued undeterred. "Kiernan came to me before he left and he asked me to go with him. I could na' do it, though. I railed at him for leaving you when you needed him the most. For abandoning his responsibilities like a frightened child. And aye, he was frightened. I'd never seen him more skittish and unsettled in all our years. When it was clear I wasn't going with him, he gave me two envelopes and told me to call Joel. He never said where he was going or why, but he made me promise to do two things. One, to look after you. And two, to contact Charlie's ma and tell her what had happened. Apparently he'd been talking to her, keeping her up on how Charlie was doing."

"Can't be true. His parents kicked him out. Disowned

him."

"His da kicked him out, Hash. His ma was as much a victim as Charlie."

"He beat her, too," I said, Kiernan's insistence on protecting Charlie becoming much clearer.

"Aye. And when Kiernan found out, he told Charlie he would do anything he could to get his ma out, too. But while he worked on it, he would make sure Charlie's ma knew how her son was doing. So before Kiernan left, he made me promise to find Charlie's ma and get her out."

"And did you?"

She nodded. "Where do you think Mela came from?"

I didn't realize I'd lost my balance until I was tipping into the helm and trying to right myself. My beautiful, calm, caring Mela. She'd cared for me as a mother these three years and now I knew why.

"Did he make you promise not to tell me?"

"No. But I knew if I did, you would be angry with her whether she deserved it or not because Kiernan had deemed her worthy of being saved and yet he'd abandoned you."

I wanted to argue, opened my mouth to do so, then stopped. "You're probably right."

"I know I'm right, because it's what *I* thought. For a long time. Even after I brought Mela on. After a while, I realized everything Kiernan does is for a reason. He has a kind heart and the impetuousness of youth. It's a dangerous combination. He doesn't do things out of malice or spite, but he sometimes makes bad choices because he doesn't have the experience to know better. It was our Kiernan, the Kiernan we both love, who made sure Mela made it someplace safe. Hard as it is to accept, that is the same Kiernan who left you and me. I've heard his reasons – why he felt as if leaving was the only choice – and now I'm at peace with why he made the decisions he did."

I raised an eyebrow.

"I'm not telling you anything, Hash. One of these days, you'll let him tell you or you'll walk away for good. You

83

already know what Kiernan wants."

I can't run away from you anymore, Erik.

I didn't reply. I didn't know what to say to her, let alone
what to think of Kiernan Callaghan anymore.

Chapter Eight

The first time I read an email in the middle of the ocean I couldn't believe technology had come so far. Thanks to a state-of-the-art satellite system used for navigation, we had Internet, phone and television.

I didn't check my email often. With my parents and uncle passed away and no siblings, it was rare for family members to contact me. My circle of friends had shrunk quickly after I'd packed up the business and taken off with Kelle.

Most of my friends from home had gotten married, had kids and moved up in their careers. It was a path I had excluded myself from when I signed on to *Trini's Passion*. I wondered if I would've wanted those same things if Kerry had stayed and the fire had never happened.

So when I opened my email, I expected the usual assortment of creatively-titled spam and a smattering of messages from friends but not much else. I scrolled down the screen quickly, checking off the emails to delete, and came across a message from Victoria at SSA Capital, my insurance company. I had to read it twice to insure I was interpreting it correctly. When my impressions didn't change after the third or fourth reading, I sat back in my chair and ran my fingers through my hair.

"Shit," I said aloud.

They were going to give me my money. Every penny of what the building, boats and equipment had been worth, including interest for the long delay. In addition, there was the extra payout awarded by the South African government for being the victim of a violent hate crime. They were going through final approvals, but she expected the sum to be available just after the new year.

I was going to have to decide if I wanted to rebuild or take the money and liquidate the company, but the money was mine, whatever decision I made. It added up to eleven point five million rand, two million US dollars, or one point oh four million British pounds. No matter what currency they used, it was more money than I'd ever contemplated having. If I restarted my business, I would need every bit of it.

I'd never intended the business to be a one-man operation. After my first shark dive at age seven, my uncle had let me ride along on his research charter trips. By the time I was a teenager, my uncle had converted to a tourist operation focused solely on the burgeoning cage shark diving business. I became an official part of the crew and learnt how to run the business side—marketing, finance and playing nice with government regulators, which was a skill unto itself in South Africa.

One year after Kelle and Kiernan decided to stay in Van Dyks Bay, my uncle died, leaving the business to me. I immediately made it a partnership between Kiernan and me. He hadn't known I'd done it, but we were already living together and it seemed right to me.

Looking at the sum of money they were going to pay me out, it was hard to deny Kelle's allegation about the amount of pressure Kiernan must have felt when suddenly half of the business was his. He'd been twenty years old when I'd signed the partnership paperwork. Maybe I should have been surprised he'd waited two more years to take off. I'd known then the five-year difference in our ages was more than years wide. Why had it taken me this long to understand the pressure he must have felt? The pressure I'd laid on him.

And it hadn't been just the business. He wasn't comfortable being out. Not in South Africa, perhaps not anywhere, though everyone in town had known about me. About my uncle. The decision to be out was another thing

I'd forced on him. Kiernan was everything I'd ever wanted, and I knew I didn't want anyone else. Maybe he'd never been as sure about me. Or maybe it was because he was young and I weighed him down, held him back from living the life he wanted. *Shit.* Had I ever really known what he wanted? I couldn't say for sure anymore.

Then the fire had happened and something had snapped in Kiernan that I hadn't known was close to breaking.

Thoughts snarled together in my head, trying to find purchase. There was what I'd always known to be true, and what I'd thought to be real. And what I was beginning to realize had too many layers of shadows to ever be right or wrong.

He left me. I didn't deserve him.

I couldn't run the business without him. He didn't want to stay.

I didn't want the business without him.

He didn't want me.

Did he?

Looming over all of it, Kiernan's voice echoed in my ears, the reverberation shaking me to my bones, even in memory. *I can't run away from you anymore.*

I had a feeling those words were going to haunt me.

* * * *

If I hadn't turned my light on, I might never have seen it, and it could've been lost to the mounds of clothes I discarded into a pile at the end of every shift. I stumbled into my cabin after a day of dealing with the constant upkeep of mechanical parts floating in salt water, and stopped dead in my tracks when I saw the pendant lying across my pillow. I stared dumbly at it, its meaning not registering until I had it cradled in my hands and the solidness proved it was real.

It was a shark tooth, just one of the many I'd seen on the stone beaches of Van Dyks Bay during the twenty-seven years I'd lived there. But this was *the* tooth, the one I'd put around Kiernan's neck the night of the fire only hours before he disappeared.

I'd taken the tooth to Cape Town to a jeweler and had it set in South African silver with a chain that would hang low on the chest where it could be hidden easily beneath a shirt or under a drysuit. Because Kiernan had asked for it to be set that way as soon as I'd mentioned the idea to him.

He'd wanted a physical trinket of our love that wouldn't show in public.

I'd wondered about it after he left, but he'd left everything. I'd assumed it was in the house somewhere, hidden away, discarded in a drawer, or lost under the sheets that protected the furniture from dust. Never had I considered that Kiernan had cared enough to take it with him.

Then I saw the note. It was wedged between the pillow and the wall and I could see Kiernan's tight, loopy scrawl lining the card. I looked at the note as if it was an unsheathed machete, ready to cut through to the bone if I tried to grasp it. I stood there staring at it for too long, my mind imagining all the things the letter could say, all the things I wanted it to say, versus what I expected it to say or what I needed it to say.

I finally picked it up and read, my knuckles turning white as the paper crumpled in my hand. Eight words I couldn't begin to interpret, cutting through me in a way that made me furious and desperate at the same time. I slammed the door to my cabin and stormed up the stairs to the deck.

I pitched my arm back to throw the pendant out into the ocean but couldn't go through with it. There was nothing but water surrounding us. Land was still a day away and if I threw the necklace, it would be gone forever, lost to the black depths below. I couldn't stomach that. I yelled in frustration and knew that Kelle was probably watching me from the bridge thinking I was a mad man, but that was exactly what I was at this moment.

Eight words written in his looping handwriting. *I should have asked for a shorter chain*.

What the fuck did that even mean? That he should have worn my gift proudly? That he was ashamed for trying to hide what we had? Or was he going for the whole metaphorical angle that I should have had him on a shorter leash so he couldn't have left? Or maybe he was just being a contrary arsehole and commenting on my aesthetic taste in jewelry. How was I supposed to know?

I wanted to throw something, to punch something, to scream until my vocal cords gave out, but something inside told me I'd never recover if I gave in to the anger and grief now. I didn't want to be trapped on this ship anymore, my ex-lover just one floor away, sleeping soundly in his cabin.

I didn't realize I'd fallen on my knees on the deck until Kelle's arms came around me. She tried to soothe me, whispering soft words in my ear that I immediately spat back at her with anger. But she held on until the tears stopped falling down my face. Jesus, when had I even started crying? Everything was out of sync and incomplete and through it all, the thin chain stayed knotted around my fingers, cutting off circulation, the tooth boring a hole into the soft flesh of my palm.

I wanted him to hurt like I did, but could never purposefully do to him what he'd done to me. I was ashamed of the weakness he made me feel. I leaned on Kelle all the way down the stairs. She opened my cabin door and settled me into the cramped bed, pulling off my shoes and opening the porthole to let the salty warm breeze stretch over me like a blanket.

My eyes were swollen shut, my eyelids so heavy I couldn't find the strength to look up and see if she was still in my room or if she had left me.

"For fuck's sake," she whispered, and I felt her fingers pulling at the silver chain that had left my fingertips numb. She tugged at it gently, extracting it from my grip. I heard my nightstand open and she dropped it inside, closing the drawer softly. Her lips pressed to my forehead and I felt her warmth, but couldn't let go of the thought that it was

89

someone else's lips I wanted in their place.

* * * *

Kelle maneuvered the ship down the Mahakam River, her grin spreading when I pointed out the *pesut*, a pod of gray freshwater dolphins, breaching the waves around us. We'd entered the river through a delta of mangrove trees and a growing system of shrimp ponds. It was my third trip to the island of Borneo in three years, and I marveled over how fast it was changing. Already the number of shrimp farms looked to have doubled and I hoped the government was keeping a tight hold on their growth.

A mist formed on the bridge window, but there were no indications that a storm was headed our way. It was monsoon season, but we'd been lucky so far, encountering only occasional rain in the days since Vanuatu. Samarinda, Indonesia wasn't located on the coast, but farther up the river, beyond the delta. The bank on each side was covered in short trees and brush that looked recently burned. Whether it had been a controlled burn or a wildfire, I didn't know.

The river opened up and we pushed into sight of the city. On the riverbank, the Islamic Center loomed larger than any other building around it, its four-story orange spires cutting into the clouds that hung low over the city. The port was busy today with large shipping vessels pushing past the wooden houses built on stilts sunk into the river bed, and I could already hear the cacophony of traffic, car horns and people surging through the city. Kelle bypassed the main port and made her way to a small private dock.

"When are you going to let him talk to you?" Kelle asked me after we'd finished debriefing the members of the crew who were staying on board while the ship was in port. We walked down the dock into the streets of Samarinda, where *Trini's Passion* was being scrubbed and restocked. Ahead of us Kiernan, Abhi and Ed jumped into a Jeep, heading for a day-long excursion into the mountains to see the orang-utans. We were spending two full days in Borneo before moving on to Thailand, and Kelle and I were off until tomorrow afternoon.

"I don't know if I can at all, Kelle. You seem to have forgiven him rather easily." I didn't mean it as an accusation, and it came out harsher than I wanted it to. I started to apologize, but Kelle just waved me off.

"I haven't forgiven or forgotten, but he's my brother and if nothing else, I owe it to him to listen. I'm under no illusions. Just because I hear what he has to say doesn't mean I can forget. If I don't at least take that one step, there's never going to be a chance for us, right?"

She made too much sense.

"I'm not there, Kelle. I may never be. What he did to me… Jesus, you have a blood bond with him. I still feel sick when I look at him."

"I understand, Hash."

We stopped at the end of the pier and I motioned for the minibus to hold a moment.

"Listen, I'm going to head over to one of the resorts since we have the afternoon and evening free. You in?"

"No, thanks. I'm going to head into town for food, drinks and shopping. Maybe a massage. It's been a hard week and I just want to indulge. I'll see you back on board tomorrow. Call my cell if you need anything."

I pulled Kelle into a hug and kissed the top of her head. She stiffened for only a second. Physical contact between the two of us was still strange but becoming easier. She squeezed me tightly, patting my back. "Enjoy your time off."

I caught the minibus departing for one of the main resorts and crashed into a seat, almost relieved to have the solid footing of land beneath me. The ocean had become much less hospitable with Kiernan less than sixty meters away from me no matter where I went on board.

The city was packed with minibuses and *tuk-tuks*

transporting people through the crowded streets. The traffic noise was loud, too harsh for my ears, now tuned to the rolling of the ocean and the languid purr of the ship's engine. Heavy smog hung over the city, trapping the wet heat between ground and sky.

We traveled down a main road of shops and financial offices and stopped next to a towering modern hotel, all glass and shining steel. It was expensive, well maintained and private. Exactly what I was looking for. I walked through the front doors into the cool recycled air of the lobby, heading toward the back where I usually found the hotel bar. It was a couple of hours before companies closed for the day and business travelers came wandering back to their rooms for dinner and a night of rest. I ordered lunch and a beer and sank into my seat to wait.

It was often easier to find a hook-up at the hostels or local bars, where the younger itinerant crowds gathered, but I was looking for something different tonight. I wanted the anonymity of someone passing through town like me, but with the guiltless non-expectations that came with the serious business traveler. Not to mention the beds in this hotel were probably all king-sized with six-hundred-thread-count sheets. That alone had been enough to lure me here.

The bartender and I chatted about nothing of importance as the lounge began to fill. I tried not to think of Kiernan or consider the idea that I was looking for a one-night stand because of him. But as a dark-haired man in charcoal gray pants and a loose cotton shirt, with a deliciously out of place scent of juniper, sat next to me, I didn't care what or who had driven me here. He was stunning and already my shorts tightened in response to the smile he flashed me.

"Cole Esquire-Bankston," he said, extending his hand, a sly grin on his face.

"Erik Hash," I responded. "And you must be kidding me. That's your real name?"

Cole laughed and I found myself genuinely smiling back.

"Unfortunately, yes. As you can tell from the accent, I'm also English. Even more unfortunate? I work in finance."

I groaned. "I don't suppose you're a rugby fan?"

It didn't take long—it never did for me. He paid my bill and we left the lounge, talking rugby all the way up the elevator until he unlocked his hotel room door and pushed me into the counter of his en suite kitchen, the door slamming shut behind us.

Our lips met in an intense rush as I pulled at his shirt, scattering buttons across the granite. He unbuttoned my shorts, letting them fall to the floor. We kicked off our shoes, stripping off the remainder of our clothing as we moved to the bedroom, our heated flesh pressing together.

Cole dropped to his knees, took my cock in his mouth, and I couldn't bite back the moan that passed over my lips. I ran my hands through his black hair and for a moment pretended it was Kiernan on his knees for me and not some stranger from a hotel bar. But oh God, this stranger's lips were amazing.

I could already feel the orgasm building as he sucked me off, so I pulled him to his feet and locked us into a kiss as we tumbled onto the bed. This first time was going to end quickly, but I was going to let Cole use me in whatever ways, and however many times, he wanted to tonight. I knew I couldn't scrub Kiernan from my brain, but I was sure as hell going to have fun trying.

* * * *

I woke up just as the sun was beginning its rise over Samarinda. Next to me, Cole was still asleep. I padded softly to the bathroom and took a quick shower, washing myself with the soap I realized had left that intoxicating juniper scent on his skin. I dressed in the bathroom and contemplated whether I should wake him before I left, but he was up when I opened the door and peered out.

He was standing in front of the coffee maker, nude,

scooping freshly ground Sumatran beans into the basket. "Did you really own a shark diving company?"

I smiled. "I did."

"Wow." He shook his head, a playful look in his eyes. "You know, I'm probably not like the other guys you do this with. I'm not married, not attached. I'm an actual gay chap. And, Erik, you are one of the most interesting men I have ever met in my life. Is there any chance I could get an email or mobile number from you?"

I couldn't hold back my laugh. He already knew my answer, but I had to give the guy credit for taking the risk. "Not a chance."

He chuckled, the sound so much like Kiernan's laugh that my chest hurt. "That's what I figured. Coffee before you go? Or perhaps an encore presentation of last night?" He arched an eyebrow and I lost it laughing. I liked this guy. If it had been even six days earlier I would have considered breaking all my rules to give him a chance.

"I should go." I grabbed his ass and gave him one last kiss as I walked by. "It's been lovely, Cole. Safe travels."

"Likewise," he said as the door clicked shut behind me.

* * * *

The day passed quickly. Kelle and I met for lunch in the city, and she plotted our route to Phuket while I checked in with the crew on maintenance, fuel and provisions. Before I knew it, we were at sea again, winding around the islands of Indonesia as we continued to head west and north into the Straits of Malacca.

After dinner, Mela handed me a couple of beers and chased me out of the galley. I ended up on a seat on deck watching the sunset. As Borneo disappeared in the distance, I began to wonder if I had done the right thing turning down Cole's offer to stay in touch.

"Can I sit down?"

Kiernan's sudden appearance startled me, as I hadn't

heard him approach. I motioned to the seat next to me and went back to staring at the sun as it dropped gently toward the water. The red faded slowly into a golden haze that rippled across the waves, and I thought about how few sunsets I'd seen despite the number of days I'd spent at sea. I'd hidden in my cabin too many nights, ignoring the water and sky, ignoring the beauty around me as I tried to come to terms with life without Kiernan.

That I was on this deck, admiring the solitude around me instead of hiding below, made me wonder if my newfound sense of peace had more to do with my encounter with Cole or the reappearance of the man sitting next to me.

It was Kiernan who broke the silence first. "You remember the day we met?"

I wanted to say, *'I wish I could forget.'* Instead I said, "You and Kelle were just off the winery tour and we thought for sure the two of you were going to spend the entire day at the side of the boat chumming the waters."

Kiernan chuckled that chest-deep laugh, the one I could feel in my bones. I swallowed the knot building in my throat and my voice came out rough. "You know that shark remains the biggest great white that's ever been spotted during a tourist trip in Van Dyks Bay?"

"It was a big one," Kiernan acknowledged. "You told us we were seeing something special, something not many people have a chance to experience, but I didn't know whether to believe you or if you said that to every tour you took out."

I never lied to you. I forced a laugh. "No lies. It was the biggest. Do you remember how freaked you were about cutting your forefinger on a corkscrew the night before?" I scrunched up my face like he did when he was really scared and did my best Kiernan impression, complete with lilting Irish accent. "'They're going to know it's my bloody blood in the water!'"

He laughed. "Yeah, well, I didn't want to start a feeding frenzy."

95

I rolled my eyes. "You never did get sharks."

"I got them. I just didn't believe I was safe around them."

We lapsed into silence, watching the sun set, the soft lapping of the waves lulling me.

I took a long pull from my beer and waited for Kiernan to say something. From the tapping of his fingers against the arm of the chair and the way he refused to look me in the eye, I could tell there was a reason he'd sought me out. I felt the tension snaking around him the longer he took to say it.

"How was your time off?" he asked, and I knew from our years together this was his way of working up to whatever he really intended to say, but I flinched because he didn't know what I had done back in Borneo to keep him off my mind.

"It was fine. Could you just spit out what it is you want to say?"

He took a deep breath and the words flowed out of him, like the rush of water in a storm surge. "I'm sorry I left. I'm sorry I hurt you. Someday I hope we can talk about my reasons, but I don't want that time to be now. I don't want to hide behind excuses. I just need you to know that I'm sorry and I understand your anger."

I took another pull at my beer and waited for him to continue. I was expecting his next words to be about wanting me back, but the longer we sat there, the more it became clear he'd decided to leave his declaration at an uncluttered apology.

He was delivering one message, and one message only, to me tonight—he was sorry. There would be no ulterior motives, no ultimatums. I questioned my sanity the moment the word *forgiveness* broke through my jumbled thoughts, but my heart and my head were telling me the same thing, and I couldn't fight that for long. Forgiveness was far away if even possible, but for now, I decided to believe he was sorry.

It was the smallest of concessions and yet so much more than I thought I'd ever be capable of. It didn't stave off the hurt or free me from the gutted feeling of betrayal I still felt when I was around him, but his apology was sincere and unfettered to any other expectation. It was a gift I'd not expected to receive tonight.

I wanted to hold on to my anger, but I was beginning to realize it might not have purpose anymore. Maybe I was letting him off too easy. My next words caught even me by surprise. "We were so young, Kerry."

He nearly toppled off his deckchair laughing. "We're still young!"

My lips crooked at the corner. "It just feels like I'm so much older now."

"You were always the old man in our relationship anyway."

"I was, if by old you mean the more responsible one." I meant it to sound harsh and was satisfied when it did. While I was willing to concede he was truly sorry for leaving me, a part of me wanted to make this as difficult for him as I could. I wanted him to understand how much he'd hurt me.

Kerry nodded, a smile still on his face. "Very true, babe."

We sat looking over the ocean, watching the sun's last rays disappear into the line of darkening waves. The ship rolled softly. The air was warm and intoxicating, briny, and fresh.

"Erik?"

"Yeah?"

"Can I hold your hand?" Kerry stretched his arm out, bridging the gap between our chairs.

I stared at his hand and wondered if it would still feel the same. I'd always been a physical person. Touch, to me, was everything. And Kerry's touch had repeatedly sent me over the edge.

My chest constricted and I found I couldn't talk. So I simply reached out and let our fingers twine together. The weight of his hand in mine was comfortable, warm, familiar, not as electric or erotic as it had been many years ago. I was okay with that.

Next to me Kerry hummed happily and squeezed my hand. We sat silently, watching the ocean until the sky was filled with stars and a chilled breeze came off the water. But I couldn't let go. Not yet. Maybe not ever. And it scared me to think that, but I couldn't stop the thought, now that Kerry had taken that first step to erase our long-held battle lines. There was still something between us. Whether it was rational or practical was a discussion for another time.

All I knew was, for the moment, I was exactly where I needed to be.

Chapter Nine

I never ceased to be amazed by Thailand, no matter how many times I traveled there, which had been quite a bit in my years with *Trini's Passion*. It was Ed's favorite country. He loved the food and the endless sun. For a while, I thought Ed's penchant for Thailand was also because of the women, but no. Ed was oddly and steadfastly dedicated to Trini.

Phuket, an island off the west coast, was his favorite part of Thailand. It was surrounded by rock formations jutting from the ocean, covered in leaves and vines, next to miles of white sand beaches, some developed and overcrowded, but others that were only accessible by boat and therefore nearly deserted. There were the usual palm trees, street vendors, beggars and tourist traps, but I'd come to love the endless surprises the island offered when I took time to explore it, like the rock caves and one-room Thai restaurants where none of the staff spoke English.

We were scheduled to pick up Ed's guests in Phuket on Christmas Eve. Everything came together perfectly, the weather, the operation of the ship and customs in port, leaving us nearly a half-day ahead of schedule. We sailed into Yacht Haven at the north end of the island and Ed gathered the crew together once we were docked. He announced he was going to check in to a resort and spend Christmas Day on land and we would hit the water again the day after the holiday. Then he shocked us all by offering to put up the entire crew at the resort.

I didn't want to leave the ship unmanned, so I told him I would stay behind so the rest of the crew could take him up on his generous offer. No one protested my idea. Even

Kelle gave me a sheepish grin, as if she felt guilty leaving her ship, but I wanted her to be able to celebrate with her brother.

By the afternoon of Christmas Eve, I was alone on *Trini's Passion*, a cold beer in my hand, the LCD TV blaring an action movie and a pot of noodles simmering on the stove. It didn't matter that I wouldn't be leaving the ship—this was the first Christmas Eve since I was a child I hadn't been expected to work.

My belly full and a buzz starting to take hold, I pulled out my laptop and started surfing travel sites to see what kind of competition had popped up in the shark diving trade since I'd closed down three years ago. The note from the insurance adjuster was enough to get me thinking about the possibility again.

The chance to run my own business once more and not be at the beck and call of a millionaire's hapless husband was exciting. Kelle probably wouldn't return with me—I couldn't begin to pay what Trini offered her—but if I left, Kelle would understand and support my decision. It was odd knowing that about her. She truly cared what happened to me. I suppose she always had and I simply hadn't recognized it. When I looked back, I saw many times when I should have known she didn't hate me. I'd been blind too long and in too many ways.

I was happy to find that South Africa was being careful with sharks as a tourist attraction. There were still only a limited number of licenses available and I did a silent thank you I'd decided to renew ours every year, just in case the settlement ever came through. Otherwise, I'd be looking at a three- to four-year wait for approval.

I surfed through construction companies, trying to gauge what it would cost to build a new shop on the piece of property I already owned. Then I started looking at real estate sites. I wasn't sure I wanted to rebuild on the site where Charlie had died. I looked at docks and scoped out boats and equipment, scrawling notes as I went along. I felt my confidence returning, my ideas of how to rebuild becoming more tangible by the moment.

I didn't know why I'd doubted myself. It was time for me to run my own business again. I could do this, would do this, and I'd do it on my own.

I heard a key in the lock to the main cabin door and the distinctive swish of it opening. I expected to see Kelle, as she was the only other person besides Ed who had a key, so I didn't know what to say when Kerry was suddenly standing there. I was on the couch, feet propped up on the coffee table, my computer on my lap, piles of notebook paper surrounding me divided up by to-do lists.

He chuckled. It wasn't the first time he'd found me surrounded by the tangible manifestation of the chaos that was my creative process. "Happy Christmas, mate."

"It's not..." I read the clock behind his head. "Happy Christmas, Kerry." I put my laptop on the couch and cleared the stacks next to me into a pile on the coffee table. "Come watch *Die Hard* with me."

"One, two or three?"

I raised my eyebrows and crooked my head. "You have to ask?"

He toed off his shoes and plopped down next to me, just close enough for his knee to lightly brush up against mine. "Beer me."

I passed him the beer I'd just opened and grabbed another one off the table.

We sat beside each other, drinking our beers and watching John McClane try to make it back to his wife for Christmas. Kerry was silent, and for once even his brain seemed to be turned down. It was such an unnerving change that the longer we sat there, the antsier it made me. I couldn't escape the thought that this was the first time we'd been truly alone in over three years.

"Nothing to say?" I eyed him suspiciously.

Apparently baiting him was easier for me than going with the flow.

"Just happy you let me stay," he said as he settled his head against the couch and drank more of his beer.

I watched his throat work as he swallowed, had to hide my blush when I couldn't stop the images of my dick in his mouth. Jesus, or my cock in those hands. His fingers slid against the condensation gathering on the glass. His hands were more calloused now than they had been when he'd run the shop.

It was a detail I hadn't realized I'd noticed until now.

I felt betrayed and hurt. Goddammit, it still hurt. His gratitude for me allowing him to stay made me feel guilty. He knew I didn't want him here. He was right. And that hurt, too, because at one time I'd thought I would always want Kerry at my side. But none of that could stop me from tearing further at the wound that had been reopened with his reappearance.

I put my beer down and faced him. I didn't know if it was the alcohol, or his proximity, or because it was Christmas and I had the sudden urge to drive him away so I could spend the holiday alone and sulking. But I couldn't keep my mouth shut. "I don't know if I want you to stay."

"Hence why I said I was surprised you let me." His tone was so nonchalant, my temper flared. He relaxed against the couch, his beer resting on his chest. I tensed then realized how much this scene mirrored the one between Kelle and Kerry when she'd challenged him about Charlie. That seemed like decades ago.

Asshole, I wanted to say.

Instead I kissed him, which shocked the hell out of both of us.

We pulled away from each other quickly, but our eyes locked and we were on each other before I could remember why this was a really, really bad idea. The growl that escaped me the moment I locked onto his lips was completely involuntary. I didn't know how I'd survived for so many years without this. Without Kerry underneath me, next to me, inside me.

"This is a really bad idea," he said as his lips traced down my neck and he lifted the shirt off me.

I arched back and watched him draw my nipple into his mouth, an unyielding ache surfacing and crashing within me as he took the bud between his teeth and pulled, drawing all sense from my touch-starved body. But wasn't that the point all along? "I don't give a shit," I managed to rasp.

Kerry's answering rumble of laughter was enough to eradicate any last reservations I was holding on to.

"I need you inside me now," I said as I climbed on his lap and thrust our hardening dicks together.

Kerry shook his head, and dug his hands into my hips, forcing me to slow down. "Uh-uh. I've waited too long for this. I am going to make this so slow you are begging for release by the time I make you come."

Shit, that wasn't going to take much. He ran his fingers down my chest, barely touching fingertips to skin. I rolled my hips against him and he pulled back, keeping us just far enough apart to torture him as much as he was torturing me.

"Fuck me," he said in a rushed whisper. It was a response and not a command, but I chose to ignore the difference and unbuttoned his pants before he could protest. My hand slid around his cock and he whimpered, at the same time thrusting up into my fist. Fucking hell, Kerry Callaghan was whimpering for me.

I nipped at his lower lip, letting my tongue trace the familiar contours of his already swollen mouth. He tasted like beer and hints of lemongrass and cilantro. He kissed me harder, his tongue sweeping into my mouth, wiping away the remnants of any anger I had. He lifted me and I wrapped my legs around his waist, growing harder at the feel of his cock against mine as he carried me down the hall to my cabin.

He was still as strong as I remembered. His muscles flexed under me, lean, perfected by hours in the water, unwittingly powerful, dangerous as a shark on the hunt. I pulled away from him long enough to slide out of my shorts. A wicked, yes, truly fucking wicked, smile spread across his face as I stood naked in front of him. He ran his tongue along his bottom lip and gestured at me.

"I can't decide where I want to start."

I wasn't giving up control just yet. I wanted Kerry to fuck me, needed to feel him again, if only this one last time. But for now I wanted to use him, to drive him mad for keeping his touch away from me so long. I leaned against my dresser and languidly stroked my cock.

"Erik..." Kerry groaned through clenched teeth, and fell back on the bed, his arm over his eyes.

My cock jumped at the sound of my name said so low and threatening. He was already on the edge and I was determined to push him over it.

Kerry lifted his arm and unabashedly peeked out at me, eyes glazed as he watched. His tongue traced his lips. His breath was ragged. No longer did he look like a predator, but neither was he the prey. This Kerry was different from the one I remembered.

Kerry had always been in control, but this was him barely restrained. Feral. And fucking beautiful. He slid off the bed and undressed slowly, never taking his eyes off me as I wrapped my hand around the head of my cock. I let a whimper then his name escape, stroking myself harder, faster, losing more control as he shed each piece of clothing.

His skin was a honey, golden tan all over. I imagined him stretched out naked on a towel, hot sand under him, sweat beading between his shoulder blades. But that image couldn't compete with the reality in front of me.

Kerry, powerful muscles flexing, closed the distance between us, stalking me, head bowed. He put his hands on either side of my hips, palms on the dresser, and watched me jack off. He kissed along my collarbone, the hollow at the front of my neck, and his hot breath fell in waves down my chest. I ran my cheek against his hair, hungrily taking in the scent of my ex-partner, my ex-lover. The man I... I bit the word back and thrust my groin into him. This I could handle, this closeness, his skin against mine, him buried inside me. But the other? Not now.

He was hard, slick already with pre-cum. Fuck control. I had to taste him, needed to know if he was everything I remembered. I dropped to my knees and took just the head of his dick into my mouth, teasing the ridge with my tongue. I worked slowly at the tip, taking it in with a laziness that hid how desperately I needed his salty, warm skin against my tongue. There was a sweetness to the cum as it beaded at his slit that hinted of simplicity and sun-ripened fruit, and I wondered how long he'd been in Fiji.

He tensed above me and swore under his breath. I had to take my cock into my hand to relieve some of the pressure I felt beginning to build out of control. Only when he was panting, his hips pushing his cock forcefully into my mouth, did I take him all the way in, deep into my throat until Kerry gave a strangled cry I knew all too well. That sound echoed in my nightmares.

But now it fueled me, drove me closer to the edge Kerry was already teetering on. His hands fisted in my hair, his entire body tensing as his rhythm became more erratic.

For a moment I thought that there was no way we were making it to the bed then he stilled.

"You're still bleeding deadly at that. Fuck, Erik." He slowly pulled out of my mouth, and I kept my lips around him until there was an audible pop and he chuckled. He leaned over to kiss me, gently this time, pulling me up flush against his body, the fire between us now a scorching slow burn. He led me back to the bed, pulling me on top of him as he fell back onto the disheveled sheets.

Without warning, he flipped us over, me onto my back and him straddling my hips. He pushed our cocks together and used his hand to rub both our lengths. The roughness of his hands gave more friction than it ever had. He knew exactly how to touch me from root to tip, to twist his wrist as he forced our heads together into his fist. His grip was so firm it should have been painful, but instead my balls tightened with anticipation.

He went for the nightstand drawer and quickly found the condoms and bottle of half-used lube. He shook the bottle and raised an eyebrow. A sideways smile tugged at the corners of his mouth.

"Don't judge, mate," I said, returning the smile.

Kerry growled. "The thought of another man touching you... It drives me mad, Erik."

I knew I should have been more bothered by his words, by the unguarded possessiveness I heard in his strained voice.

He opened the bottle and slicked us both, continuing a maddening rhythm of long, hard strokes followed by languid swipes of his thumb drawing the heads of our cocks together, over and over again.

Just as the pressure built to a point I wouldn't be able to return from, he took his hand away, moved down my body and lowered his mouth to my balls, taking one then the other inside his hot, wet mouth.

His slick fingers explored my hole, teasing, stretching, exploring, until I mumbled incoherently, clearly now his prey, baited, hunted and caught. I was split open by his hands, by his moans of pleasure. He had to hold down my hips to keep me from bucking uncontrollably. I'd forgotten what it was like to be seduced by him at one moment and dominated at the next. It was a deadly combination and a habit I'd never kick if given the choice.

"Please, Kerry. I need you to fuck me now," I groaned.

Kerry was suddenly around me and in me, but it wasn't enough. I was breathing the scent of his sweat, pulling my legs back to give him full entrance, his body pressed firmly against mine, his breath ragged in my ear, the groans as he pushed inside me uncoiling the desire that started deep in my groin and went like wildfire through my veins, and it still wasn't enough.

He rode me slowly at first, keeping a driving rhythm that hit exactly where I needed it to. But that couldn't last long, it never did with us. He groaned and snapped his hips, pounding into me, his fingers circled around my cock as he begged me to come for him, and that was all it took.

I had never been able to deny Kerry.

His breath was hot in my ear, his plea so desperate I was undone. I came harder than I had since he'd left, my sense of present and past skipping, shorting out, erasing the years apart and remembering only this, only Kerry. He spilled his wet heat inside me, his cock thrust deep, as he groaned one last time and collapsed on top of me, the thin layer of latex the only reminder that things weren't settled between us. I pushed the thought away and caught the whimper in the back of my throat as he pulled out, tossed the condom in the garbage next to my bed then coaxed me under the blanket. I nuzzled into his neck and he dragged me closer, making sure our bodies touched from head to foot. I waited until his heartbeat slowed and his breathing fell in a long, quiet pattern before kissing the base of his neck and whispering an "I love you" that was too frightening to be anything but the truth.

* * * *

We were still tangled together, my crimson sheets bunched between us, smelling of sex and Kerry, when I woke up in the morning. I had to extricate a half-numb arm from under him to roll out of bed. He mumbled something and turned over on his stomach, hiding his head under his arm, and fell back to sleep. I pulled the black comforter up around his shoulders, kissed him on the back of the head and padded to the shower.

I turned the water on and waited for the steam to curl into the air and fill the small space before I stepped in. My body ached. Not just from the incredible sex but also from the hours I'd spent locked in his arms unmoving, afraid that

107

even the smallest movement would shatter our tentative peace. I wanted Kerry back, I wasn't daft enough to think otherwise. I thought he wanted me, too, but hadn't that been my problem before? Making too many assumptions?

He didn't know I was moving back to South Africa to reopen the business. No matter what had happened last night, it hadn't changed my decision. There was still the small discussion we were avoiding about what had made him leave three years ago. But I didn't want to hurt anymore. I wasn't complete without him, if I was being honest with myself. I was willing to forgive just about anything if he decided to come back with me.

The pit in my stomach grew as I showered, and the sex-fueled fog of last night faded in the light of day. I couldn't just let his betrayal go. Kelle had told me he had reasons, ones she believed, even understood, and I needed to hear them out. At one time I'd believed there was nothing more pure than Kerry's heart, that it didn't steer him wrong. But I didn't know if I wanted to hear what he had to say. I didn't know if I would even be able to trust him.

Then there was my greatest fear of all, the one that had kept me locked in his embrace, dreading the inevitable post-orgasmic buzz kill. Maybe he didn't want me in the long-term partner way I wanted him. I rested my head against the tile and let the water beat down on my shoulders. If I thought any more about this I was going to make myself sick.

Fuck it. It was Christmas and I wanted to spend it with Kerry, without expectations or painful conversations. The click of the bathroom door, and the nearly silent tread of Kerry's feet on the cedar floor, only solidified my intent to let my questions and insecurity fall away. I was going to spend today with the man I loved.

The shower door opened and he stepped in, wrapping his longer body around mine and placing a kiss on my neck. His skin was cooler than the water and I shivered against him. He reached around me, increased the temperature and soaped up my body.

"What do you want to do today?" I asked, sighing happily as his rough hands worked the soap into a lather.

"This."

"By 'this' do you mean the shower, nakedness or the two of us spending time together?"

"Why do I have to choose?"

My heart jumped. I didn't want to force him to choose, and not just about today, but about the future as well. Soon enough I was going to have to tell him I was reopening the business. I didn't know if he would see my move as an opportunity to go back to the life we'd had, or if it would just be an opening he'd take to leave without the same guilt as before.

"You don't. How about we finish up, I'll make you a proper Irish breakfast and then we'll spend the day on the beach?"

"That sounds perfect, babe." He kissed me and trailed his hands down my spine to my ass before he grabbed my hips.

"Uh-uh, none of that in here." I slapped at him, swatting him away from my ass. "If we get started, we'll never leave this ship."

"Something wrong with that?" he murmured into that soft spot beneath my ear.

I held back my cringe. *I can't give you that much. Not yet.* "It's been a long time since I had lunch with you. Or swam with you, come to think of it."

A look of confusion passed over his face, but it was gone almost immediately. "All right then," he responded.

I wanted to know what he was thinking but was still too skittish to ask.

We finished up our shower, packed a day bag with food, clothes and a few bottles of wine and locked up the ship. Phuket was a popular destination for Christmas travel, especially with Europeans. It was a cheap, relatively short flight to escape the cold and rain settling into most of the continent in December. While other places around the world were ghost towns on Christmas Day, it looked like any other day in Phuket.

We stopped at a street vendor and picked up a bag of Thai deep-fried doughnuts covered in sugar and two cups of hot tea. We spread our towels on the beach and shared the doughnuts, telling stories from our Christmas holidays growing up.

"The year Kelle was ten, she a wanted an ostrich more than anything else in the world."

I nearly choked on the doughnut in my mouth. "An ostrich? You're joking, mate."

Kerry chuckled. "No joke. She'd read an article in some nature mag, *National Geographic* or some sort, that showed pictures of ostriches fighting. Vicious pictures really. Those wankers can brawl, do some real damage. Anyway, she was being bullied at the time by this group of harpies in our school." Kerry dug his hands into the sand, down to the wet layers, and started to build a castle at his feet.

I imagined Kelle as a child of ten, could vaguely remember seeing pictures from around that time. She was tiny now and would've been even more so then. What Kelle lacked in stature was made up for in sheer force of stubborn, calculating will. "I'm willing to wager these girls had no thoughts as to what they had unleashed."

Kerry looked up at me and smiled, eyes dancing. "Aye, no doubt about it. I'll get to that part. But first, the ostrich. Kelle got it in her head she wanted an ostrich to train to fight. She put together a whole presentation for our parents on where she would keep it, how she would feed it. Bless our parents, they didn't blink an eye. Told her she had made a convincing argument and they would put in a word to Santy for her. Of course neither of us believed in him anymore, but Kelle, set on her goal, knew that appeasing our parents was her ticket to that beast.

"Even though we shared a room then, Christmas Day morning I didn't even hear her get up. All I heard was a scream of delight and then Kelle yelling my name. I couldn't believe that our parents had actually bought her an ostrich. And believe me, I was kicking myself for not thinking on a grander scale when it came to my list. Kelle pulled me into the living room, past the tree, which by chance did have the remote control car I'd been asking for tucked under some branches. She told me there was an ostrich tethered in the backyard, its head buried in the ground. I didn't think it strange since many of the pictures I'd seen of those ghastly beasts were with their tiny pointed beaks buried in the sand. So why not in Ireland too?

"I got to the window and put my hands against the glass, peering out into the dark morning. When I realized what was tethered out back was decidedly not an ostrich and looked very much like a goat grazing our garden, I doubled over in laughter and began to torment her immediately. Poor Kelle. She was devastated and I rubbed it in every chance I had. Of course our parents thought she just wanted a farm animal to raise, not that she had plans of teaching the gargantuan to fight for her. In their minds, a goat was a practical idea. In the end, it didn't matter. Kelle bargained with a group of older boys, trading my remote control car for protection, in fact. And she didn't even have to steal it from me. I willingly gave it to her to guarantee her safety. Damn but she was convincing. Still is!" Kerry shook his head.

"How have I never heard that story?"

"I don't know. It's classic Kelleigh. I still tease her about it to this day."

We sat silently, building the sand castle together.

"You like her, don't you?" Kerry finally asked.

I snorted. "Aye, I do. Things changed, yeah?"

"Aye, they did. I'm glad you had each other. I always knew you two would figure it out someday. It makes me happy to see." He brushed his hands on his trunks. "I'm going to swim. Join me?"

"In a bit. I want to be lazy. And watch you."

Kerry turned and winked at me before he took off to the

surf.

I leaned back on my elbows and watched Kerry strip off his T-shirt and walk into the water. My breath caught in my throat as he stretched, muscles rippling, soft skin stretching over lean muscle, the feel of him still echoing in my fingertips.

He lifted his arms and did a low dive into the water, disappearing below the surface, the sea barely registering his presence. The only visual better than Kerry in swim trunks was Kerry swimming naked, droplets of water rolling off his golden skin. He surfaced farther out, shaking his black hair free of his eyes then slicking it away from his face. I fell back on the towel and closed my eyes, trying to quell the urge to run out there and lick the water off his nipples. I turned over on my stomach and covered my eyes, loving the warm touch of morning sun soaking into my pores.

I must have fallen asleep, because the next thing I knew Kerry was kissing up my back and in between my shoulder blades. I remembered we were at the beach, but we couldn't still be there because Kerry had never shown affection in public. But I could feel the sunshine still warming my skin and hear the sound of waves hitting the shore, kids splashing in and out of the water, their happy calls filling the air. There was sand under my fingers and the smell of aloe and sunscreen. And there was Kerry, draped over my back, his lips tracing circles on my shoulder blades.

"What time is it?" I asked, my mind still groggy, half a step behind.

"Almost noon."

I groaned. "How long was I asleep?"

He shrugged against my back. "About an hour. Long enough for me to start getting impatient."

I remembered. "You need to be entertained."

He nodded, his chin digging into my back. "I need to be entertained."

I began to rise and he moved with me, kissing me on the

112

cheek as I sat up.

"Food?" He already had our lunch unpacked and a bottle of wine in hand with two glasses balanced precariously in the sand.

We spent the rest of the afternoon that way, our bodies always in contact as we sipped our glasses of wine and watched the crowds move about the beach. We talked about our time apart, where we'd gone, what we'd done, but never about why he'd left or how I'd ended up on *Trini's Passion* with Kelle. I was grateful he didn't push it. When my cell pinged with a text in the late afternoon, I knew I was being called back to duty.

"Kelle?"

"Yeah, she's ready to start planning the dive trip tomorrow."

Kerry began packing up our stuff. "She told me Ed and his guests have a mix of experience."

"Ed and I already talked about it. He wants to divide off into two groups. The more experienced in an open ocean dive and the newbies at a reef nearer to shore."

"Ugh, you take the deep sea. Not my thing. In fact, Abhi may be interested in joining you."

I looked up at him. His green eyes were open, unflinching, trusting. I'd wondered if there was something between Kerry and Abhi, but after hearing that, I dismissed it from consideration.

"Then why don't you take Kelle with you? I won't need her on the ship and the two of you could have some more time together."

"Sounds like a plan." He kissed me again and helped me to my feet.

"What happened to the Kerry who was so petrified of PDA?"

He put his arms around my waist and drew me into his chest. "I don't want to waste any more time."

My face must have been an open book because I was momentarily thrown by how serious that sounded.

Then he laughed and kissed the top of my head. "Don't read so much into it. Just let us be what we are, okay?"

My heart sank. We weren't anything, but I didn't have the strength to point that out.

Chapter Ten

While Kelle was well on her way to becoming a master mariner, the international certification for ship captains, I was still only a licensed mariner, despite my years owning the shark diving company. I could operate *Trini's Passion* legally with that license, which freed Kelle to leave the ship in my hands and work directly with her brother for the first time in years.

As soon as Kerry had mentioned my idea, she'd beamed and nearly jumped into my arms for a bear hug. The kiss on the cheek she gave me after was the most unguarded moment we'd ever shared. "Thank you," she'd whispered in my ear.

I hoped she didn't think if Kerry and I were together again she would quickly become the third wheel. I wasn't going to let that happen. I'd always respected her. I wouldn't have brought her on as a captain with Great White Adventures if I hadn't. In the short weeks since Fiji, our relationship had become easier. It felt right to call her a friend.

"I don't get the allure of an open ocean dive." Kelle's eyebrows furrowed. We stood shoulder to shoulder, the tension between us gone, as we leaned over the laptop on the bridge.

My eyes lit up. Kelle knew how to dive but wasn't a dive master like her brother. She preferred to be above the water rather than below it.

"It's the freedom, Kelle. The silence and blue expanse. The mystery of what is below you, above you and next to you that you can't see, or that can appear at any time. It's also technically challenging. You can't let your guard down

115

for one second when you're that far out at sea. It's too easy to be lulled by the peacefulness around you and lose track of your distance from the boat or how much air you have left. Surprisingly, I think that challenge is why Ed wants to do it. That man can be such a chop, but when it comes to this he's really focused. Whatever his reason, I've found a spot a couple miles offshore where I've heard we may be able to see whales."

"The whales I can get into. The rest of it just sounds creepy and boring."

I nudged Kelle with my shoulder. "Boring my ass."

"Speaking of ass. You slept with him, didn't you?"

I spat out the *rooibos* Mela had made for me, luckily missing the laptop and splattering the window. "Excuse me?"

Her eyes sparkled, a mischievous Callaghan look on her face. "You heard me, Hash."

"I don't think that's your business, yeah?" I teased her.

"Do I need to remind you I am your captain? I'm the boss of both of you. So, mate, this is the definition of my 'business'."

"And you have no interest in this as a sister or a friend?"

"A friend? Never." She put her arm around my waist and leaned into me, planting a kiss on my shoulder.

"Hmm…" I grunted.

"Thank you for giving him to me tomorrow."

"We're not back together."

"I know. Regardless, thank you."

"You're welcome, Kelle." We talked over the plans for the dives and I remembered there was something I'd meant to ask her. "Did you tell Mela I know she's Charlie's mother?"

Kelle shook her head. "That one's up to you, Hash."

"She and Kerry are talking?"

"Aye."

"I'll let them make their peace first. Mela knows I care for her. There is plenty of time for revelations."

"That there is," she responded in a low voice, her eyes

focused on the nautical maps in front of us.

I felt her tense. "You okay, Kelle?"

"You know I prefer being on the water to in it. Just trying to remind myself it will be fun."

"It will be. And your bro will be there to take care of you."

"Bollocks. I could do this on my own."

And just as quickly, the usually confident Kelle was back, her professional persona once more in place.

We finished outlining the dive plans before joining Mela in the galley to start dinner for the returning crew members. They were happy, rested, and I knew that had a lot to do with Ed's Christmas generosity. I assumed it also had something to do with the palpable transformation between Kelle, Kerry and I. People ate quickly and got back to work, eager to complete their tasks and get to bed as it was going to be an early start the next day. Ed and his guests weren't joining us until before sunrise, so Mela finished cleaning up and said goodnight. Then it was only the Irish twins and me in the galley, picking the last of the noodles out of a large stock pot and sipping glasses of wine.

"Did you hear from the insurance company?" Kelle said between bites, dropping noodles carefully into her mouth.

I flinched. The question was innocent enough, but Kelle didn't realize it was probably the most loaded thing she could have asked me other than how many guys I'd slept with since Kerry left. I tried to sidestep it. "They're in the process of finalizing it."

She continued on, completely oblivious to my attempt at brushing it aside. "Whoa. So you're actually going to get it?"

I shrugged. "We'll see."

Kerry looked between Kelle and I, confused. "You still don't have your money from the insurance company?"

I cringed. This was exactly what I'd wanted to avoid. Kerry and I hadn't said one word to each other about the fire or why he'd left, both of us circling the topic as if it was a vial of bubonic plague with a cracked seal. "Soon."

"I don't get it. The fire was three years ago. How has it taken this long?"

Kelle raised her eyebrows, looked between us and realized too late what she'd started. She shot an apologetic look my way.

"The criminal case just ended..." I started, but Kerry interrupted me almost immediately.

"What do you mean it just ended? They did find them guilty, right?"

"They did. But it got...complicated."

Kerry stared, waiting for me to continue.

I sighed. "When it came out I was gay and you had left, and the kid killed in the fire was a teenager staying with us, the police dragged their feet and let the court of public opinion convict me instead of the ones who actually set the fire. And the insurance company refused to do any kind of a payout until I was cleared and responsibility was assigned to the appropriate party."

"Bloody fuck, Erik. I had no idea..." An accusatory glance passed between Kerry and Kelle and I wondered what that was about. But Kerry just looked at me like he was completely resigned to the fact that we were going to have this out now. "But that prejudice is exactly why I left."

* * * *

I rested my chin in my hands, trying to keep myself calm, formulating the words in my head before I said them. "I get why you were scared, Kerry. Bloody hell, I always knew why."

Were we really going to do this now?

Frustration crackled in the air between us, like a live wire we'd already stepped on and now there was nothing else to do but deal with the consequences. So I said exactly what I'd been waiting to say for three years. "What I don't get is the how. How was it possible for you to plan it weeks in advance, to change account ownership, talk to legal counsel, all while you were still…"

I ran my fingers through my hair. Somehow my temper went from zero to volcanic in less than a second and suddenly I was yelling. "…still fucking me? That's what I want to know. Until it actually happened, I didn't know you could be that cold-blooded. And that realization was almost worse than the actual betrayal. Worse than reading that paperwork. Worse than the moment I woke up and knew you were gone. Because I was sure then I had never really known you. And if everything you'd said was a lie, then everything you felt for me had to be, too.

"It took me three months before that cruel truth dawned on me. That was when I really lost it, not in the days after your disappearance. *Trini's Passion* was in the middle of the Indian Ocean the night I broke. I gave serious consideration to jumping in just to see how long I could stay afloat. I thought about cutting myself before I jumped. I wondered if the great whites from the Cape would know the scent of my blood and come take me down. Because that felt oddly poetic, to be slashed apart by the creatures I loved most in this world. Let them tear me apart because I should have known they were too dangerous to love."

I'd never told anyone that story. Especially not Kelle because, at the time, she'd have dumped me at the first port we landed in. But now, all I could see was worry on her face, maybe even regret. I couldn't look at Kerry. His sharp inhales were enough to tell me he was crying. For some reason that infuriated me more than his usual cavalier or unemotional response.

I could no longer control the fury that had been building inside me since the day he left. I gripped the table in front of me and looked up at him. His eyes were overflowing. "Don't you dare cry, Kerry! You lost the right to shed tears for me when you walked out of our house, past the burned remnants of our shop while the ashes were still hot and I learnt you were gone from our lawyer! Bloody fuck! I knew you didn't want me anymore, but you didn't even have the decency to let Kelle know you were alive."

A pained look passed between Kelle and Kerry and my stomach sank.

Kelle cleared her throat. "I knew where he was, Hash."

The color drained from my face. I was humiliated for being the chop I'd always accused Ed of being. I wondered how I could've possibly thought things couldn't get worse.

"So it was only me that you abandoned."

Kerry swiped at his tears and pleaded with me. "Erik, please don't do this."

I slammed my fist on the table, making them both jump. "Fuck you! Who else knew? How many other people did you chat with, sharing stories of your travels? Laughing about poor Hash's self-destructive streak? While you shut me completely out of your life!"

Kerry was shaking his head, muttering something about it not being like that, but I wanted an answer. I deserved an answer. "How many, Kerry? How many?"

"Everyone knew."

Everyone. Not just his family. Not just Kelle. Everyone. I didn't want to hear any more. He'd left me, then walked back into my life as if he didn't owe me any explanations.

And I'd let him.

I had to be splintering in half. My blood was ice cold and the air weighed against my shoulders, heavy, blazing, too hot to draw into my lungs without a searing hiss. Somewhere in my head, I knew heat and ice couldn't exist together, and *this*, this was going to be the moment where I shattered into cleanly split pieces that no one would ever have the patience to put back together.

Kelle turned on her heel and walked away, tears streaming down her face, back to the safety of the bridge. It was only the second time I'd ever seen her cry.

Kiernan continued to talk to me. I could see his lips moving, those beautiful lips that at one time had had the power to hypnotize me, but I couldn't hear him anymore. The waves lapping at the sides of the ship were the only sound I understood. I turned my back to him, pulled off my shirt and dove off the boat and into the bay before I could think twice about it. Kiernan was swearing behind me when I jumped, but his voice was the last thing I ever wanted to hear again.

I let the water cradle me as I swam farther away from the ship, following the shoreline until the ship disappeared behind me and I passed beyond the resorts. It was late enough that the water was quiet but still warm from the relentless sunshine of the day. When my arms began to protest, I slowed my stroke and rolled onto my back, relaxing until it was only my breath and the salt of the water keeping me afloat. Above me, the stars broke through the blackness in thick layers and for a moment I understood just how big the universe really was and how small I was in comparison, but it was way too heavy a thought. I drew lazy circles in the water with my hands. The silky caress of sun-warmed water between my fingers and across my palm brought me some measure of peace.

One more day. I would finish the dive with Ed tomorrow, help see his guests off then make my way back to the Cape. It was time to go home.

Chapter Eleven

"They've probably been in the water for an hour already."

Ed's words were muffled by his regulator, but I wasn't interested enough to care. Kelle and Kiernan had taken the smaller group of less experienced divers to a reef closer to the shore as we were steering the ship into deeper waters. I was spending the morning with Ed and two of his friends, doing an open ocean dive miles off the coast. I'd done more open ocean dives than I could count and Abhi was on the ship to assist me, so it was going to be an easy morning. We were scheduled to do forty-five minutes then return to Phuket to meet up with the other group.

I was counting down the hours to my flight. My bags were packed, and I'd purchased my one-way ticket last night after finally swimming back to the ship and calling Trini to give my official notice.

Mela was in the galley when I made the call, continuing her work silently as I laid out all the details for Trini. As I talked, I watched Mela float around the galley, preparing the meals for tomorrow. Every now and then, I would see a flicker of emotion cross her face. She didn't hide that she was listening because she knew if I'd wanted her to not hear, I would've asked her to leave. Trini was professional, thanking me for my service and assuring me Ed would have enough cash on hand to pay me out. I hung up and laid my head on the table, watching Mela dice peppers.

"Did you know as well, Mela? That Kiernan was talking to Kelle?"

"Yes," she answered without hesitation and I flinched. "Mr Callaghan sent messages to his sister and she confided in me."

"Why didn't you tell me?"

"You wouldn't have wanted to know."

True. It would have made me resent Kelle and stirred my anger with Kiernan. Two weeks ago I wouldn't have wanted to know, yet I wished I'd known before I'd slept with him.

"She never replied to his messages," Mela added.

I hadn't considered the possibility that Kelle had kept him shut out, that their communication had been completely one-sided. "Because he took her money."

Mela laid down her knife. "And because he left you."

I was an awful judge of character. I'd kept Kelle at arm's length all these years because of what I'd perceived as coldness and anger, when she had been the only Callaghan loyal to me all along. Damn those girlie bits. I'd fallen in love with the wrong Irish twin.

Ed pulled out the regulator and repeated himself, pulling me back into the present. "Are you sure you don't want to stay on?"

I'd told Ed this morning about the email from the insurance adjuster and that this would be my last trip on *Trini's Passion*. He seemed oddly melancholy about the whole thing considering how little time we'd spent together, but I couldn't be bothered to worry about the old coot. Kelle would quickly find someone to replace me. There was never a shortage of willing and able help when it came to private charters.

"It's time for me to get back to my business, Ed. I will miss this ship." It was the truest thing I could say that wouldn't hurt his feelings, so I left it at that, patting him on the shoulder when I stood up to check on Abhi's work with the safety lines.

We were all under the water before long. I tapped my air gauge, reminding them to check it often and pointed to the two safety lines we'd dropped from the back of the ship. They hung deep in the water, acting as a visual marker and tether to the ship.

It was easy to get lost in the vastness of an open ocean

dive if you didn't pay attention. I raised four fingers then five and pointed at my watch before circling my thumb and finger for the 'okay' symbol. The four dispersed in opposite directions, moving slowly. The feeling of weightlessness was more intense in an open ocean dive and it could be a life-changing experience. Despite my anxiousness to get on that plane, the opportunity to enjoy this last dive was kind of a thrill.

I rolled lazily in the water, staying close to the ship and the surface so I would be available if anyone needed help. The water here was a striking deep blue, almost royal blue in the places where it wasn't cut through with the rays of the sun. I focused on my breath and let the water hold me.

Through my drysuit, I could feel the chill of the ocean, but it was nothing like the often frigid waters of the Cape. There, the currents from Antarctica swept up to the southern coast, bringing penguins and sea squalls, as well as providing the most hospitable waters in the world for great white sharks.

Abhi swam into view, pointing at one of Ed's guests then signaling up. Apparently she was ready to go back up top and Abhi was going to escort her. I gave him the okay sign and swam with them over to the ladder to help hold it in place.

They climbed up and I was left watching Ed and his friend slowly make their way back up to the ship. The current picked up for a moment and I held onto the ladder. The currents were slightly more insistent than I was used to, but nothing to worry about, especially since I knew this place had been used for dives for years.

There was a yank on the ladder. I looked down, but both Ed and his friend were still making their way up unaided. Another pull and I looked up but couldn't see anything besides the amorphous shadow of the ship. I swam up hard, past the ladder, aiming for sunlight. A cold dread spread through me. When I broke the surface, Abhi was there, peering over the side of the ship, his face drawn and almost completely white.

"There's been an earthquake," he yelled down. He was waiting for me to respond and I didn't know what he wanted me to say. I pulled my mask off and the regulator out of my mouth. Then realization slammed through me.

"A tsunami," I called back, deathly certain I was right.

The expression on his face was all I needed.

I pulled myself up the ladder, grasping desperately at the rungs as my thoughts cascaded one into another, following the implications to a place I couldn't go—not yet—or I'd completely shut down.

"Stay by the radio, I'll get them out of the water." I didn't know if the earthquake had just happened and there was the potential for a tsunami, or if the earthquake had happened hours ago and the dangerous wave had already passed us by on its way to the coast.

"When was the earthquake?" I yelled so he could hear me over the railing.

He reappeared above me. "Three hours ago in Indonesia."

Then we were already too late.

"The tsunami hit Phuket about an hour ago," Abhi said, confirming my worst fear. "At least, I think so. Reports are still erratic."

I swung my leg over a rung to help me hold onto the ladder and checked my watch. "How big?"

Abhi looked sick. "Ten meters. Maybe more."

I swallowed the bile that burned in my throat. My stomach rolled and adrenaline flooded my body.

If Kerry and Kelle didn't pay attention to the signs, or if they were unable to get to high ground fast enough, there was no way they could outrun a tsunami that big.

* * * *

I paced the deck, constantly looking at Abhi on the bridge. We were waiting for the all-clear. The last broadcast from land stated that the water was receding from the coast, but they didn't want any non-emergency vessels to approach the shore yet. And it wasn't as if there was a functioning port anymore for us to moor to.

It didn't matter that we were miles out in the ocean. I was fighting the urge to jump over the side and swim in. I needed to be on the ground looking for Kiernan and Kelleigh. My Irish twins. We'd already tried calling their cellphones but very little was working right now. Intellectually I knew it would be complete chaos but had no idea what that meant in reality.

I tried to convince myself that every person who'd worked on a beach or on the ocean for any number of years knew about tsunamis and how to spot them. But there was no early warning system to speak of in the Indian Ocean. Downstairs in the main room, Ed and his friends were glued to CNN, watching everything unfold live. The wind carried snippets of reporters' voices, each update increasing the estimated number of dead. Right now, it was in the thousands, but I knew it would be more, many times more than what they estimated, if initial reports of a ten-meter wave proved to be true.

I heard the startled whispers when the first images came out of Phuket, the soft wail from Ed's friend when they showed the resort they had stayed in only last night. Mela's expression, as she stood at the top of the steps, was trapped between an instinctive desire to help and the reality of how useless we all were. A highball glass shattered when Ed finally passed out after drinking too much Fijian rum.

For at least the tenth time in the last hour, I leaned over the railing and heaved. My stomach was empty, the spasms painful, and I felt gutted, completely empty inside except for the pain that spiked through my heart every time I thought of Kerry and Kelle. If I could have, I would've gladly returned to last night, even though I'd been humiliated and angry. He'd been alive then.

I tried to convince myself they would've known what was coming. They would've seen the receding water and run either into the hills or into a tall building. Then I panicked, thinking about the possibility of a wave that large taking down a building. Was that even possible? I began to hyperventilate. All around me the ocean swayed gently, the sun shone brightly and the world was falling apart.

I was falling apart.

A hand dropped softly onto my shoulder and I spun around.

"We can move."

I hesitated for a second, while I processed that Abhi was telling me this because he couldn't drive the ship, but I could. I ran for the bridge. As I drove, Abhi manned the radio, trading messages with people on land and water. We heard there was another tsunami coming then that warning was canceled. We heard the sea around Phuket was littered with debris and impassable for any large vessels. We heard that small vessels ran the risk of being smashed and sunk as cars, trees and bodies flowed from the land out into the ocean. We heard the clinics were overrun and makeshift morgues were being set up across the island because there were too many dead to hold in one place. Then we heard that cell service was working and Abhi didn't say anything about reaching Kerry or Kelle, so I didn't ask.

Only the sound of the engine really registered. I rode the ship hard, harder than it had ever been driven, so I listened for any signs it was going to give out. I only needed *Trini's Passion* to make it to the island. It took two hours to reach a place where we could see the devastation of the wave.

Abhi nearly collapsed, my hands gripped the wheel and my vision swam out of focus. We passed Khao Lak first. The city was gone, trees uprooted, the beach full of debris. The devastation went far beyond what we could see from the water. I was shocked to see streams of water, blackened by dirt, oil and I could only assume blood, actively running from the land back into the ocean. Based on what we knew, it had been seven hours since the wave had hit.

On the deck Ed looked up at me, eyes reddened by tears and too much rum, and shook his head in disbelief. He was thinking the same thing I was—how could anyone have survived this?

I drove slower down the Thai coast, aware that I needed to watch out for the piles of debris that swirled in the water. Inexplicably there were patches of land that appeared untouched, where palm trees still swung gently in the breeze and cabanas sat nestled into the hills. Then the coast would return to chaos, trees shredded, buildings collapsed and gutted, boats pushed onto land, cars and furniture and papers floating lazily in the waves.

At some point, I stopped seeing the destruction around me and shut down. It was as if I was in a video game and my mission was to make it to the shore, but the obstacles became more complicated and massive the closer I got.

Abhi touched me and I stared at him coldly, trying to figure out why he thought he had the right to do that. Then I realized that didn't make sense, but before I could apologize he spoke, "They're telling me there's one marina with an accessible dock on the other side of the island."

We passed by the beach where Kerry and I had spent the morning—fuck, was that only yesterday?—lounging in the sun. The port where we'd cleared customs was now only white sticks jutting out of the water with demolished cars and motorbikes squeezed between the splintered posts.

We continued down the eastern side of the island. A heavy silence hung over everything, almost drowning out the sound of wailing voices. I couldn't decipher whether the quiet was in my head or all around me. I closed myself off to the smells, the sights, the thud of debris against the hull. I pushed back thoughts of what might be floating underneath the swirling brown and black water. When I felt as if I was going to crack open from the pressure of keeping it all out, I spotted a single dock ahead and maneuvered the boat around. Mela worked with the deckhands to secure us and handed me my cell and a backpack of water and supplies as I ran for the shore.

Chapter Twelve

I ran toward the beach closest to the reef where they'd planned to dive. It was my only thought. My only direction. I passed a makeshift tent made of blue tarps. Under it, bodies were lined up, some wrapped in plastic while others sat in the shade waiting to be cataloged. I tried not to look, tried to forget the blue facemasks that covered the mouths of the workers and the white scrubs stained with black smears.

I didn't know how I knew, but I wasn't going to find Kerry here.

It was a feeling that had crept insidiously through me since coming into view of the devastation in Phuket. I'd stuffed it down, confusing it for irrational hope, but it held, warming me inside, and each step through the rubble only strengthened my resolve that what I was feeling was right. My Kerry was alive.

I sprinted through the streets, adrenaline pumping through my veins as I warred between this irrational surety of survival and an unspeakable panic of what would happen if I was wrong. Only later would I be able to piece together what I'd seen in that run—the impromptu memorials, hastily drawn signs with pictures put up by those seeking loved ones, the clinics full but clean, cars crushed together as if the hand of God itself had rearranged them.

Everywhere there was death—humans, dogs, rats, felled trees. And within the carnage, humanity came together with words of comfort, coordinated search teams, bottles of water passed between parched lips. Hands, bodies, words shaking with tremors of fear, adrenaline, relief.

I'd never seen anything so horrible. These were the

images I would sort through and try to deal with later. Images I would carry to my grave. And I suddenly had a much stronger understanding of how soon, or sudden, that end could be.

I slowed to glance inside every clinic I passed, searching for that distinctive head of black hair and golden skin. As I got closer to the beach I stopped in my tracks, paralyzed by the thought of knowing for sure. I'd always thought the adage of knowledge being power was about strength and invincibility.

But standing near what used to be a concrete sea wall dividing a resort from the street, the cabanas crushed and tossed together like a demented Lego set, I understood that knowledge also had the power to harm, the power to break down. And I thought about the sharks and how, even armed with the same knowledge, Kerry and I had always felt differently about them and how dangerous they were. I thought about Christmas Eve and holding Kerry in my arms, the solid warmth of him wrapped around me protectively, so alive and so real, and I held onto that memory because I couldn't believe that would be the last time I would touch him. I was shaking, but that inner calm continued to push through my veins, strengthening me.

I heard pounding steps behind me and turned just as Kerry threw himself into my arms, knocking the wind out of me and almost collapsing us to the ground. He burrowed into my shoulder and wept in jagged sobs. I existed only for him at that moment. Felt only him.

There was no strength left in him and I worried. It seemed that the only thing holding him together was me. It was frightening, too much to take in, a burden that should have been too heavy, but I would've gladly borne it forever if it meant he'd always be with me. I held onto him until my arms ached and my legs shook from keeping him standing. But I wasn't going to let go.

Behind him, I heard voices. The same intuition that had told me Kerry had survived whispered the dark knowledge that I wouldn't find his twin with him. Fuck. I tried not to picture her, to hear her voice in my head. I tried not to think of the heartfelt apology she'd given me this morning as I turned my back to her. Because my pride had been worth more than her friendship. I'd needed a day to be pissed, time to let my anger fade. We'd always had tomorrow. Until we didn't.

I tried to calm the voice within me saying he and I would never be close enough. I inhaled the scent of his sweat, that which was only Kerry, and was comforted that the water couldn't wash away who he was. I heard a whimper slip through his mouth when I shifted my weight and realized he was hurt, which snapped me back to the present. I cradled his head in my neck, my eyes clamped shut, forcing the destruction around us out of my thoughts. I kissed his cheek and his ear before I settled my chin gently on his head.

"Where does it hurt, baby?"

"Nowhere." He spoke so low it was hard for me to hear him. "Everywhere."

I opened my eyes then and looked over his shoulder. I knew what to expect but it didn't make the scene any easier. Ed's three friends had grouped together, hesitant, whispering to each other. Kelle was nowhere in sight. I stared, blinked, forgot how to breathe.

"Let me take you back to the ship." I brought my arm under him and let him sag against me as we walked. There was a pronounced limp to his step and a white bandage peeked out from under his track pants. He wasn't wearing shoes. I motioned for Ed's friends to join us. "The ship is docked nearby and in perfect working order. Let's get you all back there so you can rest."

The man—I couldn't remember ever thinking it was important to know his name—handed me a pair of flip-flops. "The doctor gave these to Kerry to wear, but he wouldn't let us touch him."

I was able to stuff down a sob, but the tears flowed over

my cheeks and down Kerry's face where they left streaks in the dirt caked along his jaw. "You stubborn asshole," I whispered under my breath then spoke to Ed's friend again. "Help me hold him up while I put them on."

Kerry didn't protest this time. He had used up all his energy waiting for me to come. On the way back to the boat, we barely talked. We were all shell-shocked. I was amazed any of them had survived.

One of the women kept repeating that Kerry had known I was coming for them. I'd never felt so honored yet uneasy, guilty I hadn't been there when he needed me the most. It took many times as long to walk back to the ship as my initial frantic search had taken. We worked our way through the rubble, my muscles stretched to the limit under Kerry's weight. We came to the dock just as the sun was starting to set.

Ed let out a wail, grateful and pained, as his friends boarded. He climbed to the dock and helped me carry Kerry to his cabin. I could see the question in Ed's eyes, the name neither one of us wanted to say aloud, but I couldn't pull myself away from Kerry's side. I wasn't going to bring her up when he was this far gone. I just shook my head and said, "Thanks, Ed. Go take care of your friends." Ed pulled me into a ferocious hug then shut the door to the cabin as he quietly slipped out.

Kerry curled up on the bed, his eyes clamped tightly shut. I sat next to him and stroked his hair back from his face. A low, pained moan escaped his lips as he pushed his head into my hand. The guilt was a physical thing, rolling and twisting inside me. I'd failed him. Failed Kelle. I kissed his hands, his neck. I'd never been more thankful and restless in all my life. "I'm so sorry, baby. Just lie there and let me take care of you."

He turned onto his back and laid his forearm over his eyes. His clothes were covered in the same black sludge and dust that seemed to have coated everything the water had touched. I tugged at the corner of his shirt, "Do you want me to save them?" He shook his head and I left him long enough to grab scissors from the galley.

I started at the collar and clipped down. His chest had already bloomed with bruises and I had to hold back my gasp.

There were deep purple contusions spread across his left side, and red starbursts of blood just below the skin. I clipped the T-shirt off his arms and pulled it out from under him. He groaned with the movement. I froze and let him settle into a more comfortable spot before I continued. Then I moved down to his track pants, pulling the cloth away from his hips and cutting it down the leg.

I moved carefully at his left leg, which was bandaged from the foot almost to his knee. A large purple blood blister spread across his thigh. I was amazed he'd been able to walk at all. What had happened to him?

Kerry was alive. That was enough for now.

I carried him into the bathroom. Kerry was bigger than me and yet his body fitted too easily into my arms. He curled up, arms interlocking into a fierce grip on his chest, and tucked his head under my chin. His whole body was tense, in pain and way too vulnerable.

He didn't close his eyes as I arranged him in the shower and stripped my clothes off before stepping in next to him. He watched my every move and yet saw none of it. I shivered under his glassy stare. Kerry was lost in his head and I hoped I could be enough for him to want to come back out.

I considered storming Ed's room to use his black marble tub so Kerry could soak away the ache that would be tormenting him tomorrow. But I knew Kerry needed peace, head space, something to ground himself to eventually. Ed would only hinder that process. I turned on the water, making sure it was warm enough before I let the spray envelop him. The initial shock of cold water raised goose bumps on my skin.

I tried to shield Kerry from the worst of it, but I doubted

he knew where he was. His eyes were unfocused, his black hair slick with grease and sweat. His body shivered, but the water was warm, so I knew it wasn't from the cold. He balled up on the tile, his knees drawn up to his chest, and lolled his head back to catch the spray of water across his face. He winced every time the water hit one of the many shallow cuts that lined his body. I washed him slowly, letting the water do most of the work. He didn't lean into my touch, but he didn't fight it either.

Slowly his body uncoiled, responding to the warmth and, I hoped, to me. Eventually, the water pooling at his feet turned from black to clear. I didn't know how much time had passed. I was wreaking havoc on the hot water tank but everyone else could fuck off.

When we were done, I wrapped him in one of my red towels and carried him back to the bedroom. It was only then that I took the time to really look at him. To explore his body. I wanted to make sure he had no major injuries.

He was covered in tiny, shallow cuts that pulled apart every time he shifted on the bed. But the bruising was the worst—large swathes across his ribs, legs and hips were swollen, distended, unnaturally hued. He'd obviously been battered by something or possibly pinned for a while.

I reminded myself that Ed's friend had said they'd seen a doctor, and I used that to tamp down the panic that threatened at every nerve ending in my body, because he was still watching me. He'd told Ed's friends I was coming for him. He had trusted me to save him. I wouldn't let him down.

His fingernails were ragged, as if he'd been clawing at a brick wall, so I picked up his clippers and smoothed them down. The bruises were darkening with each passing second. I ran my hands down his sides, gently pressing on his ribs, watching Kerry closely for any hint of discomfort.

I'd unwrapped his ankle to wash away the dirt and sweat. One long cut snaked its way up the length of his left leg. It appeared to be superficial, but I didn't know what medicine, if any, the doctor had given him. I would pick up antibiotics tomorrow just to make sure.

His feet were ripped raw in places and I worried about that more than anything else. How long had he gone without shoes? Walking over splintered wood, shards of glass and twisted metal in water that carried sewage, blood and God knew what else. He would need a tetanus shot if they hadn't already given him one.

He curled onto his side and I breathed a sigh of relief to see his back virtually untouched. He finally closed his eyes and began to shiver, so I dragged the comforter over us and pulled him into my chest protectively. Kissing the back of his neck, I whispered promises I didn't know if either of us could keep.

My mind was just starting to catch up to the reality of what had happened when sleep began to tug me under.

"I don't know where she is, you have to help me. I don't know, I can't find, she has to be here somewhere, but I can't..."

I was wide awake as soon as I heard his voice. I pulled him as tightly to me as I could, until I worried I was hurting him. He was half-conscious and I couldn't decide whether to wake him or not because I was no longer sure which was worse — reality or his nightmares. All I could do was try to comfort him and hope maybe he would find Kelle alive in his dreams.

* * * *

I rented us an apartment in the hills above Phuket City. It was one bedroom, small, clean, sparsely furnished, in an L-shaped building built around a courtyard of tropical flowers. There wasn't an agreement on paper about how long we would stay, just a handshake and an exchange of baht that equaled only a couple of rand a month to me but was priceless to Kerry.

It was one day after the tsunami, and the surreal events

135

of yesterday had faded into the brightly shining sun that mocked and amplified the destruction around us. Power was slowly returning to the island and a spate of NGO disaster responders commandeered the streets in their officially sanctioned T-shirts.

The pleas for help in locating missing relatives now lined the fences and buildings downtown. Kerry and I went there first, with a picture of Kelle tucked into a sandwich bag along with a listing of all the cell numbers on the ship.

He moved slowly and I knew the pain was almost debilitating, yet he insisted on walking. We stopped by a clinic and picked up antibiotics and a strong pain medication. The nurse inside informed me that everyone who couldn't verify a tetanus vaccination had received a booster. Kerry walked with me as I ticked items off the list.

We needed food and water, a motorbike, our luggage brought from the ship to the apartment, and to close out our final obligations to Ed and find *Trini's Passion* a new captain, then to officially register Kelleigh Callaghan as one of the missing. Perhaps then I would hear what had happened, how they had been separated, but as of this morning, Kerry still wasn't talking.

It was evident at breakfast that Ed had heard the story from his friends. He was uncharacteristically quiet and a pained look crossed his face every time his eyes slid by Kerry. Not that Kerry noticed. Or maybe he did. I was becoming less sure of what to expect from the surviving Irish twin.

Every time I looked at him, I expected to see eyes that were wary or devoid of emotion. It was what I saw repeated ad infinitum across the faces of the survivors. There were exceptions to that, people who were already organizing and cleaning, leaving the past in the past, and their faces wore a different mask — acceptance, defiance, forced optimism — but that didn't fit him either. He stood apart from the other survivors. The best I could say was that he was determined. Fractured, but not broken. And I had no idea what to do with that.

For once, I couldn't see the gears turning in his head. He took in the carnage around him, unflinching, as if somehow this level of violence and upheaval was normal, to be expected. His apparently easy acceptance of it chilled me, made me wonder again why he'd left South Africa. I had wondered how Kerry had been able to walk past the burned-out remains of our shop. Now I knew. He shut it all off, closed himself down, and it frightened me.

We barely talked that first day, but he wasn't distant either. He kept his hand in mine as we worked our way through town, ticking more items off my to-do list. We ate, not a lot, but enough, and he gulped water. His eyes were clear and his strength seemed to build throughout the day instead of waning. This wasn't the Kerry I'd known three years ago — so unsure of himself — and I wanted to weep with gratitude. My Kerry probably wouldn't have survived. I had no doubt this Kerry would.

137

Chapter Thirteen

Two days after the tsunami, we stood at the dock and watched *Trini's Passion* depart, a new captain at the helm. Abhi was now a permanent member of the crew and Ed was a drunken, bawling mess of a man who kissed and hugged us both fiercely before pressing a thick envelope into my hand and telling me to call him soon. There were scratches down the sides of the ship from our initial push through the debris to get to the island, but a mechanic deemed the ship seaworthy and Ed was taking it back to Australia for repairs.

"I think I'm ready," Kerry said as the ship cleared the island and passed out of our view.

I searched his face, but his eyes were clear, his shoulders confidently set, and I couldn't find any sign he was lying to himself or me.

"Okay," I replied and took his hand in mine. We'd reported Kelle as missing this morning and the government agent had asked if we'd walked through the tent morgue to see if we could identify a body. I still didn't know if Kerry was holding out hope that his sister was alive, so I didn't press the subject. We now had unlimited time in Phuket, and more than enough cash, if the size of the envelope from Ed was any indication. I wasn't going to push him to do anything he wasn't ready for, but Kerry continued to amaze me with his clear-headed strength.

We didn't have to search for the makeshift morgue—we could smell it. The government was in the midst of moving the bodies to refrigerated, secured facilities, but most of the dead were still lined up under sheets of plastic in a blue tarp tent.

We slid the offered face masks over our noses and mouths and walked the lines. I tried to focus on the faces and ignore the horrific injuries—missing limbs, bloated skin, wounds that sliced past the muscle into organs, blackened blood and bodies that were unrecognizable as human. I wanted to fold into myself and disappear from the sights, the rancid smells, the sheer indignity of these circumstances. No matter how they'd lived their lives, no one deserved to end up like this.

With each step, panic swelled inside me. I wasn't going to leave Kerry to do this on his own, though, so I breathed through my mouth and tried to detach from what I saw, tasted, smelled and heard. I focused on Kerry's touch, on his hand pressed into mine. His calloused fingertips against the back of my hand. Easy. As if we'd been this affectionate in public for years.

It took the rest of the morning before we were sure her body wasn't under that blue tarp. We got the location of the place where some of the bodies had been moved so we could check there as well.

"I don't think we're going to find her there," Kerry said as we rode away on our motorbike.

"Let's still go."

I felt him nod against my back.

Kerry was right, she wasn't there either. Whatever Kerry knew about Kelle's final moments, it was enough for him to think finding her body wouldn't be easy.

We spent the next three days in a similar pattern of searching in the morning, sleeping in the afternoon and spending evenings in the city, helping to clean up debris. It was hard work and we were physically exhausted every night when we fell into bed, but even that couldn't stop Kerry's nightmares. He called out for her in his sleep, begging for someone to help him find her. I would hold him close and whisper in his ear, trying to drive back his fear. He didn't remember the dreams when he woke in the morning, and I guessed his real memories were more painful than any dream could be.

Five days after the tsunami, we were working with an NGO hauling garbage when one of the workers asked if we were coming to the beach for the party that night. Kerry and I looked at each other dumbly, as if neither of us understood what she meant.

"For New Year's!" the girl said.

I'd lost track of the date, but even if I'd known it was the thirty-first, I probably wouldn't have put two and two together. I told her we hadn't decided and looked to Kerry for an indication of what he wanted to do. For the first time since the tsunami, he looked lost. I let the topic go and worked until the truck bed was filled. I waited until we were alone in the truck, taking the debris to the dump site, before I broached the subject.

"What was it that caught you off guard back there?"

I knew enough about Kerry not to ask if he was okay, because he clearly wasn't. That dismissive question would solicit just as dismissive an answer from him. Kerry was hunched over in the passenger seat, his elbow against the window, his head leaning on the frame.

"I'd forgotten New Year's Eve was tonight, but I guess that's not really surprising. I just suddenly remembered what I hoped to be doing New Year's. I mean, before all this happened."

"What was that?"

"I was going to fly to South Africa to spend it with you."

It took me a minute to realize what he was saying. I hadn't told Kerry I was planning on leaving for home as soon as our dive was over. Before the tsunami, the last words we'd said to each other had been about anger and betrayal. That fight felt years old now, not days, as if my anger had long ago been muted by the passage of time.

But as soon as he brought it up, the memory of that night ground at me, unresolved. It was a living thing standing between us, whether or not we wanted to acknowledge it.

I knew we would have to confront it eventually, but the immediacy was gone.

"How did you know I was going back there?"

"South Africa is in your blood, Erik. Just like sharks or the water of the Cape. That's why I was so surprised to run into you in Fiji. I thought for sure you had the business back up and running years ago. So when you said the settlement was just coming through, I knew you were going home."

"I hadn't even made my final decision then!"

"Yeah, well, you try to fool yourself. I know you better than *you* know you."

Of course he did. I was surprised at the surety of that thought. Kerry's heart never steered him wrong. With as much time as Kerry spent analyzing things in his head, he had to know me better. Then he surprised me by dismissing the topic with a shake of his head, saying, "Let's go to the beach tonight."

I grabbed his hand across the cracked leather seat. "Okay."

* * * *

The beach blazed with light. Bonfires were scattered down the sand, shadow people coaxing the flames higher as if they were pitting element against element, willing the fire to beat back the water. Kerry and I made our way through the crowd, saying hello to the travelers, NGO staff and locals who should have been strangers but who were now irrevocably tied to us.

We stood at the edges of the water, letting it lap against our toes. A warm breeze came off the ocean that called to me, reassuring me that the worst was over and calm had returned. But I knew the sea too well now. This respite wouldn't last, yet I couldn't imagine being away from the water. Even Kerry seemed drawn to it. He put his arm around my waist. "It's beautiful."

I simply nodded, not trusting my voice.

Bottles of beer, cold despite the incessant heat, were

passed around. At some point, we'd become separated in the crowd, and I didn't know how he was doing in this crush of people. Someone started playing a Bob Marley song and I found myself really smiling for the first time in what felt like years.

We'd been close to the water all week. On an island, it was unavoidable, but we weren't far from where I'd found him and I still didn't know which beach he'd been on when the wave came. He'd also been surprising me all week, so when I walked around a bonfire to find he was the one with the guitar in his hands playing Bob Marley, I had a moment where everything felt as if it was going to be okay.

I grabbed a couple of more beers and took a seat next to him in the sand. He turned his head and winked at me. I was completely lost to him, but he probably knew that already.

As the hours passed by, and midnight and a new year drew closer, most of the partiers moved inside the hotel nearby. The fires simmered instead of roared, illuminating the beach in pockets of low, flickering light. Conversation and laughter became muted, but the feeling of hope never flagged.

"Those are called Kongming lanterns, or sky lanterns." Kerry pointed to a line of paper domes being carried out from the trees. "Someone was telling me about them. They're lit and then released. The act of releasing one is considered good luck. Symbolic of letting our troubles go."

Our troubles.

You can rebuild.

I can't run away…

The two of us were intertwined in ways I didn't know how to unravel, even if I wanted to.

We sat side by side on the beach and watched them light the lanterns. People left the safety of the fires and went to the shore to claim a lantern. There were murmured whispers, shouts of joy, tears. So many tears, but not all of them sad. Then upturned faces, cast in the glow of fire, of life, as the lanterns floated into the night.

"Let's go," I said pulling him up.

I motioned to two of the lanterns and a man came up and offered me his lighter. I lit mine, held onto it as the warmed air inside began to lift it in my hands. Then I lit Kerry's. The gold reflection of the lantern intensified the green of his eyes.

I saw Kiernan Callaghan, the man I would love for the remainder of my days, whether he chose to spend them with me or not, and I realized I wouldn't stop fighting for him. For us. I looked at him and smiled as I released my lantern. It lifted gracefully into the sky and over the water, the candle inside flickering but never going out. I made a conscious decision to forgive him.

I'd lost sight of my conviction that Kerry's heart was true. Someday I wanted to know more about why he had left. The reason could not be forgotten, but I knew enough about Kerry to know he had done what he knew to be right. For that he deserved my forgiveness. The past didn't matter. I was letting go of that old anger tonight.

I turned and kissed him, lightly, softly, and the response of his lips against mine was immediate, moving with me. Warmth, light and Kerry — they were all I needed to survive. He pulled back, stared into his lantern, gave it a gentle kiss and sent it off.

The line of lanterns stretched high into the sky and over the ocean. The fire beneath the paper skins danced, leaving a trail of reflections on the water below. I grabbed Kerry's hand and pulled him into my arms, putting his hand at my lower back, and started to dance. He laughed, that chest-deep chuckle that went straight to my heart, and swayed with me. I snuggled into his neck and kissed his collarbone. It had been days since we'd really touched each other. Christmas Day. A lifetime ago now.

"Is it 2005 yet?" I asked.

"Don't know. Time seems to matter a lot less to me now."

"I was asking more because I'd like to kiss you."

"You can do that any time, babe."

"Even out here, yeah? In public?"

"Aye, I'm already dancing with you. I think people have the general idea about you and me."

"And that doesn't matter to you?"

"It never should have in the first place." He leaned down and kissed me, gently at first, just touching our lips together, then more insistently. He tasted of beer, coconut milk and Kerry. Always Kerry. He lingered against my lips, our breaths syncing together, our bodies fitting against each other, familiar and comforting. He pulled me tighter into his chest and whispered a confession into my ear. "I'm sorry I haven't been better for you."

I struggled with how, or if, to reply, because a part of me needed to hear that apology, whether Kerry believed it to be one or not. I also knew what had happened to us hadn't been only him.

"I didn't give you a choice back then. Didn't realize how much I was asking of you. I should have known." When Kerry started to protest I stopped him, put my hand across his mouth, and smiled. "Either way, it doesn't matter. We have time to talk about what could've been different. But at this moment..." I waggled my eyebrows at him. Tonight we needed to celebrate, to experience how lucky we were to be alive and in each other's arms.

He burst out laughing. "You did not just wiggle your eyebrows at me, Erik Hash. Really?"

"Aye, I did. It's my mating dance."

Kerry chuckled and pulled me toward our motorbike.

"See, it works."

"Tonight you can have whatever you want, babe."

He climbed onto the motorbike. I settled behind him, my hands around his waist. "Gentleman's choice, I suppose?"

His answering laugh rumbled through me. "You're not a gentleman."

"And that's why you love me."

I rested my chin on his shoulder.

"It's one of the reasons. One of the many, Erik. And I do love you. Never stopped." He turned, kissed my cheek, "Happy New Year, babe."

My heart raced out of control from his declaration and my reply was out before I could stop it. Because it was the one thing I still knew to be true.

"I love you, Kerry. Happy New Year."

Chapter Fourteen

"She went on a walk down the beach."

I guarded my reaction carefully, afraid that any sudden movement would silence him. I shut the book in my lap, and waited. It was another sunny morning, just as every morning had been since we sailed into Phuket. Kerry sat at the table, a cup of coffee in his hand, his glazed eyes fixed on a memory I couldn't see.

It had been seven days since the tsunami, two days since New Year's. Sunday had come again. Just like the sun, the days continued to appear, whether we wanted them to or not.

"We'd finished the dive early. Ed's friends were less than amateurs. They bored so easily that Kelle and I were frustrated. It was a lot of work for little pay-off, in our view. They wanted more of the beach. They wanted frilly drinks and to gorge on a lunch buffet. So we packed up the gear, docked the boat and went. But she was antsy and the thought of sitting on a beach for four hours drove her mad. So she went on a walk down the beach. It was that simple."

I kept quiet. Kerry drank from his cup and stood to refill it. He leaned against the counter and met my eyes. Sad, tired and yet determined. I couldn't look away.

"I was fading in and out of sleep, Ed's friends were in the water, and there was a little girl next to me talking loudly to her parents. She was so insistent that the sheer annoyance of it was enough to drag me awake, and then I heard her say 'tsunami' and I was instantly aware. I sat up and looked out to sea and knew she was right. I ran down the beach trying to find Kelle, but I couldn't see her in the crowd. I had to trust that she would know the signs as well. So I grabbed Ed's friends and we ran for the nearest, tallest building and we climbed to the top, eventually ending up on the roof of the hotel, where we could see the wave approaching.

"I've never been more terrified than while watching that wall of water barrel down at us. It became more and more massive as each second passed and the roar of it was deafening, but not loud enough for me to miss Kelle's shout as she sprinted down the beach toward the hotel."

"Jesus Christ, Kerry," I swore under my breath.

He stared into his cup and took a drink. His voice wavered, but he didn't stop. "There were two other people with her and I watched them run and I was sure they were going to make it, because I couldn't see any other outcome. But the water moved faster. So much faster than I ever would have guessed it could move. One moment the wave was out at sea and the next it was swallowing her up and there wasn't any time to see it coming because it was just there. After that I'm not sure what happened.

"I have these…pieces I keep trying to fit together, but I'm not sure how much is memory and how much is nightmare. Maybe the two are interchangeable. I don't know. I'm pretty sure Ed's friend pulled me out of the water as it filled the bottom floors of the hotel. I was trapped, I think, and I still can't figure out how I got down there, but the water was unrelenting. That I can't forget. The wave was just the beginning. It felt like the whole world was going to disappear under that water and everything would be ocean. I remember thinking that and laughing, because even if that happened they couldn't win. You were out there with a boat and you wouldn't let me die."

Then he changed the subject so quickly, it took me precious seconds to realize he wasn't talking about the tsunami or Kelle anymore.

"We'd been receiving death threats for months, but I never told you. I didn't want you to be scared and I was sure it was just teenage pricks playing a prank. But the last death threat detailed what they planned to do if we faggots didn't close up shop and leave town. They gave an ultimatum, a deadline, and then, the part that finally got through to me, made me realize they were serious? They included pictures of Kelle, and threatened to rape her until she was bleeding and pregnant with their bastard children because she was no longer an innocent, not with me as her brother.

"Fuck. It was so vile, so violent that I knew without a doubt they would do it if we stayed. But I couldn't make you leave, and I couldn't make Kelle leave. She was just starting to date that rugby player from the Cape. And she is so stubborn, she refused to leave just as I knew she would. It was risky leaving you there, but I didn't see any other choice. I knew you wouldn't be alone. I was sure the people of Van Dyks Bay loved you, and would protect you no matter what. I thought if I left, then maybe those homophobic arseholes would leave you alone.

"So I took my name off our accounts and completed the paperwork to revert all our business assets back to you. I talked to Charlie and convinced him it was time to move on, that I would help him get somewhere better. But the bastards didn't wait! I had two more days before the deadline when they set fire to the shop and the boats, when they killed Charlie. And I was so scared I didn't think. I just left. I drained the shared account with Kelle, because I couldn't take anything else from you, you'd already lost too much, and I left. I drove to Cape Town and flew out that morning, first to the UK, then down to Oz when my permits came through, New Zealand for a while, and I've been in Fiji the last two months. I didn't want to leave you, Erik. Bloody fuck never. I didn't know what to do. And when I realized I'd made the wrong choice, it was too late, and you'd moved on. I didn't think you wanted me anymore. Why would you? I'd left you. And I hurt you, killed Kelleigh. I'm so sorry, Erik. So sorry…"

He was sobbing, the words coming out in choked gasps. His eyes were fixed on mine. I could see why he'd been so silent this week. He'd been examining these two horrific events, trying to find a reason why they'd happened, and the only connection he could find was himself.

He'd decided to take complete responsibility for events he'd never had any control over.

I was shaking my head no, he wasn't right, not about this, then my heart broke with his next words.

"How could everything I did to save you, to save Kelle, have gone so wrong?"

* * * *

I was still reeling from the details of Kelle's death and Kerry's rushed confession, but somehow I managed to find my legs, stand and move. I crossed the room in two steps, taking him into my arms. He collapsed into me, sobs racking his body, his tears soaking my T-shirt. I clutched him tightly, holding him up, just as I had only a week earlier when we'd found each other again. It felt like years had passed in that week.

But I couldn't cry with him. Not yet. I was still too stunned by the sheer brutality of it all. And that water, the water that had saved me so many times, it had taken away what Kerry loved most in this world. That loss could not be forgotten, never forgiven. Kerry fought the demons of the choices he'd made, and I fought the demons of my indecision. I'd spent the last three years floating on the ocean to escape, to ignore that there was something more I should be doing, until the ocean had come roaring back to me, forcing me to act. I felt betrayed by the water, by the one thing that had always been my solace, my home.

I continued to be numb, for a reason I didn't understand yet, and for a betrayal that I knew was irrational. I couldn't cry. Not for Kerry and not for Kelle. Because that meant giving in, surrendering, admitting I didn't have control.

And if I didn't have control and Kerry didn't have control, what chance did we have of making it?

Kelle had been wrong. It wasn't that I didn't care if I lived or died, it was that I thought I could control it, that I could control my destiny, my death. Mourning Kelle meant I wasn't in control, and I couldn't admit that with Kerry shattered in my arms.

I lifted and carried him into our bed, keeping contact. I protected him when he lost control, for the first time showing me just how damaged the years had left him. He cried into the afternoon as the Thai heat built around us, but we didn't let go of one another. He passed in and out of sleep, fitful and brief, until finally he woke enough to eat a bowl of rice and drink iced tea.

"Thank you," he rasped.

I kissed him on the forehead. I didn't know what to say.

That night was the first where he didn't search for Kelle in his dreams. We slept curled into each other and neither of us moved.

But it was the only night of peace we had. As soon as Kerry's nightmares faded mine began. I would wake in the night with the sound of rushing water in my ears, of teeth ripping apart flesh, and the incoherent thought that if I stayed in Thailand, the great whites would follow me here, and the only way to protect the dead was by going home.

When I woke each morning, the image of blood in the water tattooed to my eyelids, I swore nothing would make me go home. Not without Kerry. As long as Kerry was here, searching for Kelle, I would be here with him.

* * * *

Things changed between us after that Sunday. Kerry's mind continued to spin. He didn't talk about what kept him up at night. My recurring nightmare became more vivid each night, the shark attacks more brutal, and the faces of the dead ones that I recognized, but didn't want to name. We slept fewer and more erratic hours, we ate less, talked to each other less, and as time went by, we stopped touching each other completely.

Months passed while we awaited the identification of the dead. Kerry gave his DNA for comparison and we waited for a call. We didn't need jobs, the money Ed had given us could sustain us for years in Thailand, but we had nothing else to focus on, so we kept working on the clean-up and rebuilding, refusing to accept anything in return.

We were singular in our drive to do everything but deal with what had happened between us before the tsunami, so many years ago now that it seemed like it shouldn't be important, but it was. And it was killing the relationship, killing us, but I didn't know how to stop it.

"Maybe it's time to go home," I said to Kerry. It was April and I sat in front of my laptop, trying to figure out how much longer I could hold off the insurance company before I had to make a decision. Returning to my business was no longer the most important thing in my life, but I worried I was losing the person who was.

If this had been the first time I'd brought up the idea of leaving then I might have been nervous about Kerry's reply. But this was the third time and I was finding myself growing more and more worried that Kerry was stuck and didn't know how to move on.

"Ireland to see your parents, or South Africa. The States for fuck's sake. I don't care where. We just need to go."

He didn't even look up. "I can't do it, Hash. I can't leave her here."

Hash. He'd called me Hash. Shit, I was losing him.

"You've done everything you could do for her. It's up to science now. There's a chance they may never find her body. What happens then?"

"Then I'll die here, too," he said flatly.

I stopped breathing. Fury spread through me like wildfire. It was the strongest emotion I'd felt in months and it consumed me. "What the bloody fuck does that mean? Are you threatening to kill yourself?"

Kerry faltered, and I saw desperation in his face for the

first time since the tsunami. He was actually considering suicide. How could I not have known how low he'd gone?

"I don't know," he finally answered, his voice barely a whisper.

I ran my fingers through my hair, hoping to buy time, to figure out just the right way to convince him. Of what I wasn't quite sure. We couldn't continue living together and yet completely separate. Something had to change. "Please, baby, please just listen to me. I'll stay with you as long as it takes. We don't need to go anywhere, we can stay here. But something has to change. You're unhappy. I'm unhappy. We can't keep doing this."

His voice was so quiet, I had to process his next words twice before I realized he'd actually said what I thought he had said.

"Maybe what I need is for you to go."

I thought of my nightmares, sharks sawing away at thigh bones, blood flowing freely, turning the water around them black, black like the tsunami sludge. I felt as if I was going under, no longer able to hold myself afloat anymore. I heard the sea breaking on the shore outside the window and expected to see that wave barreling down on us, even as high as we were in the hills. But I couldn't understand one word of what Kerry had just said to me. Kerry looked at me, the desperation wiped away by a sneer. His visage cold, unemotional. Otherworldly.

"It's time for you to go, Hash."

I wanted to scream at him, flip him off, drag him into the bedroom and fuck sense into him or suck the pain away. The last thing I thought I would do was leave him. But I was tired of fighting, tired of waiting for Kerry to make a decision I didn't think he would ever be able to make.

I turned my back to him, grabbed my passport and walked out of the door.

Chapter Fifteen

It was December again before I knew it. Summer in the Cape. This was usually my favorite time of year. I knew that this year would be different, though, because there was no way to avoid the reminders of where I'd been last year at this time.

December twenty-sixth hadn't just marked my loss, but the loss of many more than any of us had anticipated. When I thought of how many people were still grieving, still wondering if they were going to find their loved ones' bodies, I had to push it down to avoid collapsing into myself. I woke from nightmares, breath and heartbeat ragged, with the swell of adrenaline and hopelessness that filled me running through the body-littered streets of Phuket, desperate to prove to myself that I was going to find Kerry alive. The panic of December twenty-sixth was forever forged to my DNA.

I knew from Ed that the Callaghans had finally given up the search for Kelle's body, but he didn't know what had happened to 'that sweet boy Kiernan'. His twenty-seventh birthday passed without note. Just the mention of his name was enough to send my heart into my throat.

It had been eight months, three weeks and six days since I'd walked out on Kerry.

The rebuild of the shop was almost complete. It had been winter when I'd returned, so the construction had waited for the spring and in the meantime I'd bought a boat and cages, hired a crew and reintroduced myself to Van Dyks Bay. I'd moved back into the house I'd shared with Kerry and tried to ignore his ghost, but it was everywhere I looked—in the painting of the Cliffs of Moher we'd bought on our one trip to Ireland to visit his family, to his flip-flops carelessly tossed into a corner the day before he left—the house was an inescapable time capsule of the days before and after the fire.

I'd thought about selling. The market was on a high and I could have made even more money selling the house and property my shop was on, but I'd felt sick any time I'd thought of really leaving the place. I wanted to stay. I'd learnt from the brave business owners of Phuket how much honor there was in rebuilding.

A community lived or died by the people who resided there, and I loved this place too much not to be a part of it. That much Kerry had been right about. South Africa was in my blood. This water was in my blood.

I thought often of Kelle, of her life and the friendship she had given me, even when I hadn't considered her a friend. I tried not to grieve for the time we'd lost because of her stubbornness and my inability to see her for who she really was, but I finally did mourn for her. With that came a new unease about the ocean. Some might have called it a healthy respect, but, either way, I wouldn't let the fear drive me away again.

The sharks and I came to terms immediately. Despite my nightmares, great whites were not vicious creatures.

"Only one more dive and we're ready to head back," Abraham yelled up to the bow of the boat where I sat chatting with a family visiting from Canada.

I moved back to the wheelhouse and waited for the all-clear before starting up the engine. It had been a good trip today. The visibility had been clear and we'd had three separate sightings, uncommon for warm summer days, as the great whites seemed to prefer cold water. Happy tourists equaled happy tour operators, which equaled more business for me, and I was already running close to capacity. Soon I would need to decide whether to apply for an additional boat on my license and begin the search for another captain. But I wasn't ready for that yet.

Abraham appeared in the doorway. "It's a beautiful day. After this group let's take the boat back out, past Dyer Island."

I nodded. Abraham and I had started spending afternoons at sea. I looked forward to our time together. He was the only family I had left. And today there was something weighing on me that I needed to talk to him about.

* * * *

"How long have I known you, Abraham?" We spoke in Afrikaans, Abraham's first language and my second. The words still felt unfamiliar on my tongue, even after eight months back home.

"Your first time with the sharks was my first day working for your uncle."

I tried to recall the faces of the people I'd met that day, but no matter how hard I tried, I could only see my uncle and my first glimpse of that shark gliding up beside the boat. I couldn't recall Abraham's face among the crew. "How did I not know that?"

"You were there," Abraham answered dryly.

"I know that, yeah?" I laughed and drank my beer. "I don't remember you. Not that day."

"You were seven, Hash. Feeding chum to sharks. I thought your uncle was crazy."

I wrinkled my nose. "Looking back on it, I think he was."

Abraham broke into his high-pitched laugh, the one that left me laughing with him every time. We sat in the bow of the boat, our feet kicked up on the railing as we drank beers from the cooler Abraham kept stocked in the new shop, ready for our afternoon sails.

The ocean rolled around us, lulling me into a sleepy peacefulness that could only be duplicated on land when I was in Kerry's arms. I must have flinched at the thought of Kerry because Abraham's hand was on my arm, a reassuring touch, one to remind me I wasn't alone in this.

Abraham looked lost to the rolling waves and his thoughts. "I miss Ron."

I didn't know where the realization came from, but as I watched Abraham's face flicker at the mention of my uncle it was as if all the missing pieces fell together—as if with the appearance of his gray hairs following so close on my uncle's death, and his fierce protective nature of Kerry and me, I should have known all along. I didn't know why it had taken me this many years to see it. "How long were you two lovers?"

I had to give him credit. He barely reacted, even as my world realigned itself in a pattern that suddenly made much more sense.

"Until the day he died." Abraham smiled widely. I felt a surge of gratitude and love for the man next to me, who had been a better father than my own.

"I don't know why it took me so long to see it. I'm glad he wasn't alone."

We sat in silence, looking back at Van Dyks Bay. From this distance the town looked tiny, but I could see the house my uncle had lived in his entire life and the new shop that had been completed with the help of neighbors I'd thought had been happy to see me go.

"Before you ask, he always planned on you taking over the business. It and the house were always meant to be yours. He loved you."

I rested my head on Abraham's shoulder. "I know."

I didn't ask why they'd never been out with their relationship. Kerry and I had experienced enough prejudice. My uncle and Abraham had been an interracial gay couple during Apartheid years. That answer was the easy one. What I really wanted to know was how they had stayed together all those years despite everything that had conspired to keep them apart.

"You kept in contact with him even when he was gone?" I asked, finally getting to the topic I hadn't touched on for eight months but now desperately needed an answer to.

Abraham knew whom I meant without needing to ask. "Of course. All of us did," he said, confirming that everyone had been in contact with Kerry after he disappeared. Abraham held up his hand for me to wait when he saw my brows crease in frustration. "We sought him out. He wanted to punish himself for leaving. Then as we started to contact him, one by one, I think he realized we cared more about him being okay than why he'd left."

I'd never been able to get past the hurt I felt about him leaving, never considering if he was in pain. I'd forgotten Kerry's heart was never wrong. I'd fought to know why he'd left, but only for vindication, not for any concern for Kerry's own welfare.

"Recently?"

His face was drawn, worried. "No."

I sighed. "I know I can't pinpoint the moment where everything went wrong because it wasn't just one moment. But that almost makes it worse, because now I know that we had many opportunities for things to be different and we fucked them all up—one right after the other, again and again. I've never stopped loving him. I hated him just as much, maybe more, for a long time. It was cosmically unfair that he never stopped loving me. All those years he gave up because he believed it was the only way to keep me safe. Shit.

"What am I saying, though? I don't know that he does love me anymore. He told me to leave. That it was time for me to go."

"Are you sure of that? That he forced you to leave?"

I could barely get the words out. "No. Not anymore."

Abraham shrugged. "He did what he thought was right. As did you."

I stared out at the open ocean. Today was a calm day, the waves low and rolling. The sun shone down and a breeze kept the heat at bay. It should have been a perfect day.

I turned to Abraham. He was smiling, already having

come to the same conclusion that was just dawning on me.

"I've been a fool, yeah?"

* * * *

Two hours later, I was back at the house, stripping off my boots and tossing my clothes, now stiff with sweat and salt, into the washing machine, before walking into the kitchen to pop open a beer. I paused to pick up the mail and immediately noticed the large package with a return address of the court. I ripped it open before I spent time considering what the contents might be.

A bundle of papers, held together with a large metal clip, fell on the floor, landing with a hard *thunk*. A single typed page remained in the package. The letter stated that upon recent completion of the criminal and civil cases, they could not return originals submitted by Mr Callaghan, but were able to provide copies of the material for his record.

I bent to pick up the packet, thumbing through the pages. They were the death threats from the men convicted of burning down the shop and killing Charlie. There were many more notes than I'd expected. Six months' worth. Initially spaced apart then more frequent and violent as the date of the fire drew closer. I read through them, my hands shaking harder each second.

The letters were littered with grammatical errors and misspellings, the carelessness of an increasingly disjointed mind. When I finished with the last one threatening Kelle, I understood why Kerry had made the decision to bolt. This more than explained Kerry's emotional withdrawal in the weeks before the fire.

Even knowing the men were in jail, reading the letters was enough to have me rechecking the locks and windows, but it didn't help me understand the one thing I still couldn't understand. Why had Kerry forced me out of Thailand?

I'd run through our last conversation a million times in my mind. But no matter how many times I played it over, I couldn't get past the realization that this time I'd been the one to run away. I tried to tell myself that coming home was different than leaving, that Kerry had forced me into a decision. But that wasn't true. I'd used the out he'd given me, just like he'd expected I would, because he knew I couldn't deal with being in Thailand anymore. I'd abandoned Kerry when he needed me the most, just like I'd always been furious at him for doing to me.

I watched the clock tick to midnight.

Eight months, four weeks...no, that meant it had been nine months. Nine months since I'd walked out of our apartment in Thailand with nothing except my wallet and passport.

I couldn't make it one more day.

Chapter Sixteen

It was a long way to fly when I didn't know what I'd find when I landed. I was scared, tired and worn down, but never more sure of anything I'd done in my life.

The *tuk-tuk* dropped me off at the building entrance. I crossed the lawn, like I'd done too many times before to count, and walked through the garden to the building perched on a hill overlooking Phuket. I didn't know if Kerry even lived here anymore, but I didn't have anywhere else to go.

The lights inside the small space were off and I waited for a sign to tell me Kerry was still here and hadn't moved. It was late, well past bedtime, and the same white cotton drapes swung lazily in the breeze of the open window.

"How did you know?" a voice behind me said.

I froze.

"Erik," he said, his voice softer this time, less surprised, "how did you know?"

I didn't have to turn around and look at him to understand that the thing keeping him here had been settled. The pixie-like face that in my dreams was no longer suffering but finally at peace. "I didn't know. Not for sure."

Kerry walked up behind me, hesitated, didn't say anything else. He took a deep breath. His voice was still shaky when he unlocked the door. "Come in."

It was harder to walk across that threshold than I'd thought it would be. Kerry's voice held no malice or judgment, only acceptance. As if he'd been expecting me. And I felt guilty for that. I'd been the one to leave and yet Kerry invited me into his home without hesitation. I hadn't been nearly as

welcoming when it was him in this situation. Kerry flicked on a light, dropped his keys on the table and opened the refrigerator.

It had been one year since he'd unlocked the door on *Trini's Passion*, three hundred and sixty-three days since the tsunami, nine months since I had left, and here we were, together again in Phuket for Christmas Eve. So many things were the same, but things couldn't have been more different or unsure. Then he turned the corner, a beer in each hand, and I finally looked at him—no, saw him—for the first time in years.

I remembered the man I'd fallen in lust with seven years ago. I recalled the years of him working by my side, believing in the business as much as I had, believing in me. I thought about the death threats and the choices he'd been forced to make, that I'd forced him to make. I saw the years ticking away in my head as the challenges of the world etched themselves into his face. He was still so young, with many more years to live and love, and I wanted to be there for every one of them but couldn't be sure anymore if he wanted the same from me.

I hadn't come here to think at him though, I'd come to act. So I flew across the room and swooped him into a hug, burying my face into his neck, drinking in the sun-sweet scent that was Kerry. He stiffened, but I held on.

"I'm sorry," I mumbled to him, knowing those words wouldn't be enough but that was where I needed to start.

"Bloody hell, baby," he replied. The beer bottles clinked together as he closed his arms around me.

I kissed his collarbone. He exhaled and relaxed against me. He put the beer bottles down on the table, then pulled me tighter into him, wrapping his arms around my back in an embrace I couldn't have escaped from even if I'd wanted to. I felt his cock swell against my own and I nudged us together, a question more than an answer. He laughed, that chest-deep laugh that vibrated through my bones, and nudged me back. That was all it took.

Before I knew what was happening, Kerry's hands were pulling my head back for his kiss. He was insistent, testing the limits of my control, maybe to see how far I would let him go. I gave in and let him take what we wanted. I'd come to his door to grovel, to win him back, and I wasn't going to fuck this up again. As soon as I softened in his arms, his kissing slowed. He parted my lips gently with his tongue.

Why had it taken me this long to come back to him?

"I need you to be inside me." Kerry's voice was gravelly, strained, and I couldn't hide my surprise.

I shook my head. "This isn't about me. I need to do this for you. Tell me what you want and I'll give it to you."

He pointed to his head. "I can't be up here anymore. I need to just touch. To be. I need you to bring me back."

Christ, I was going to lose it before we even made it to that point. I'd only fucked Kerry a handful of times in the years we'd been together.

I jerked when I felt his hand pass under my waistband. He gripped my cock and stroked it gently while I removed as much of my clothing and his as I could without breaking contact. I kissed around his ears and down his neck, lavishing attention on the hollow at the base of his throat, as we fumbled our way to the bedroom.

He threw his head back and moaned, gripping me tighter in his hand. If he didn't let go soon I was going to lose it. I dropped to my knees and pushed him onto the bed, spreading his thighs wide. I kissed up the inside of his thighs, working my way up until I was tonguing his balls into my mouth. He cursed under his breath and leaned back to grab the lube and condom from his drawer.

I took him all the way into my mouth, drawing him into my throat, savoring the silky texture of his cock against my tongue. I slowly pulled off him and took just the tip inside, sucking gently at it then releasing. I repeated the motion until he was writhing under my hands.

I took the bottle of lube from him and slicked my fingers. I slid one finger inside him slowly and pressed gently on his prostate.

"Bloody fuck!" he cursed as he looked down at me, his eyes hooded. His mouth was open and his tongue licked around his lips as he watched me. I couldn't stifle the groan as he bit down on his bottom lip and pushed against my hand. I slid two fingers in, opening him, and he thrust his hips, trying to force more than just the tip of his cock into my mouth.

I smiled mischievously and held him down. I took him all the way into my mouth at the same time I slid a third finger inside him and he bucked wildly underneath me. I couldn't wait any longer to be inside him.

He pushed himself back on the mattress and pulled his knees up, opening himself to me. I rolled the condom on and slicked myself then him, paying him extra attention because I knew this would not be comfortable for him. But hell if that was going to stop me. If he wanted me inside him then I would give him that.

He was blissed out as I put my cock to his hole and began to push past the muscle. With one hand, I guided myself in and with the other propped myself up so I could lean over to kiss him. I could still taste him in my mouth and the mix of his pre-cum, his tongue and my cock pushing farther inside him was almost enough to unravel me.

When I was seated completely in him, I stilled, raining kisses down his jaw, on his chest then taking each of this nipples, one at a time, into my mouth. I could feel him beginning to harden again under me, but I waited until he moved before I withdrew then sheathed myself again.

"Oh, fuck, Erik. Fuck me now," he growled through clenched teeth and I couldn't hold back anymore. I slammed into him, my own moans filling the room as I lifted his hips until his legs were wrapped around my waist. I pounded into him again and again, angling to hit just the right spot inside him. His eyes cleared, focused, pierced through me. Alive and with me on every thrust.

I took his rock-hard cock in my hand and stroked it. I

could feel his climax building and held my own off, biting my lip until I drew blood, until I felt him clench around me, his seed spurting in jets over my hand and onto his chest and mine. I let go then and pushed inside him as far as I could go, emptying myself into him.

I pulled out carefully and tossed the condom into the trash next to the bed then rolled out of bed to get a towel. I knew the second we were cleaned up and I was back in bed I would fall asleep, and I wanted him tangled in my arms and legs. I wanted to protect and possess him, just like I always had. But there was a new feeling of pride and belonging that filled me. I only hoped I wasn't too late for Kerry to want those things too.

* * * *

"Happy Christmas," I said as we lay in bed, his head on my shoulder and one leg thrown over mine. We'd slept through the night, neither of us waking with the remnants of a nightmare, which seemed like a small miracle unto itself. I kissed him on his forehead and handed him a box wrapped in silver paper.

He grinned and ripped the paper away gleefully. He popped open the box and stared at the shark tooth necklace inside.

"After I left, I didn't know what to do with it," I admitted. "So when I moved back into the house, I put it in my nightstand and forgot about it. And then one night I brought someone home with me." The wince from Kerry was almost enough to stop me from continuing, but he needed to know this part as much as I needed to confess it. "I opened that drawer and, well, quite honestly, I lost it. Probably freaked the guy out. But I didn't really want him anyway, he was just a stand-in for what I'd convinced myself I couldn't have, so it was a relief when he made a quick excuse and bolted. Never thought I would be the psycho gay guy who cries before sex."

Kerry chucked softly next to me.

"Anyway, I couldn't sleep after that, so I drove into Cape Town and parked the car in front of the shop of the jeweler who'd made the first chain, and I waited there in the street until he opened his doors. And then I asked him to do something for me. Look underneath the necklace."

Kerry lifted the leather pillow the necklace was mounted on and out tumbled a mass of South African silver.

"I asked him to make me chains and mounts of every size—necklace, choker, bracelet, and earring. I hoped I would see you again, and when I did I wanted to make sure you knew it would be on your terms. I didn't give you a choice before and I won't make that mistake again." I turned on my side and played with the pile of chains. "Of course, it's your choice if you want to wear it at all. I fucked up when I left. I know that. And I'm hoping you can forgive me. Whatever way this goes, I'll accept your decision. But I'll never stop loving you, Kerry Callaghan."

A tear trickled from the corner of Kerry's eye, but I couldn't read him. He held the shark tooth in his hand, idly playing with it while the wheels turned in his head.

"They found her."

I breathed a sigh of relief. "I assumed that's what you meant when you asked how I knew."

"I got the call yesterday. She's been buried not far from here for almost a year."

"That's good."

"Yeah, it is."

We lay there, silent for a long time. Then Kerry turned his head on the pillow and looked at me. "I bought you something, too. I wasn't as sure as you that I would ever see you again, but I bought it anyway, hoping that maybe, someday, I would have the guts to find you and give it to you. So I suppose it wasn't intended as a Christmas present, but I'd like nothing better than to give it to you now."

Kerry padded out of bed to the wardrobe and palmed something from inside his jacket pocket. He knelt down next to the bed and put his arms on the mattress, studying me with a faint smile.

I smiled back. "You're beautiful, baby. You know that?"

His grin grew wider. "Flattery will get you everywhere." He chuckled and I melted. "So here's the deal, Erik. It appears that you and I and the forces of nature have all been working overtime to keep us apart. But as I see it, there's safety in numbers. So you and I, we need to agree on exactly where this is headed and team up already. And I'm hoping that maybe you'll be willing to set aside your plans for ours.

"Because I want to marry you, Erik. I want your home to be our home again. And I want to be tucked inside our shop every day while you go out on the boat because, really, no matter how you try to convince me how lovely they are, I'm still scared shitless of those damn sharks. But I understand why you love them, and I want you to be able to share your passion with others. I want to laugh with you, and drink lots of beer, and have mad sex, and maybe one day talk about kids, because I know you'd be a great dad.

"You're in my bones, Erik. In my blood. I want to celebrate that, revel in it. We keep finding our way back to each other for a reason. It's not a question of if I want you, because that's already been settled. It's a question of when and I want it to be now."

"Okay."

Kerry's face lit up. "Okay?"

"Yeah, of course okay. How the hell could I say no to that?"

"Then let me do this properly. Erik Ronald Hash, will you do me the honor of being my husband?" Kerry opened his fist and on his palm lay a plain, wide silver ring. "It's made of silver from Thailand. This country adopted me and looked after me when I needed it the most—it's a part of me now. As soon as I saw this ring, I couldn't get the image of it on your finger out of my mind."

I couldn't see past my tears as Kerry slid the ring onto

my finger, then pressed his lips into my palm. My heart thudded in my chest as I thought about bringing Kerry home to South Africa, of making him my husband. I remembered the day fate had pushed us together again in Fiji, of how unsteady I had been on my feet from so many months at sea. I'd been adrift then and in the nine months since leaving Kerry. Now I could feel the sea change, feel my world righting itself, anchored in all the good ways by the silver ring on my finger.

Epilogue

Five years later

I stabbed myself for what had to be the third time making breakfast, this time hard enough to draw blood. I yelped and dropped the knife, jumping back to avoid the pointed end plummeting toward my foot. I stifled the swear words sliding off my tongue, hoping that I hadn't made enough noise to wake Kerry's parents.

Kerry chuckled and wrapped his arms around me from behind, taking my left hand into his to study the seeping wound. "Ag, man, can't you make even one meal without maiming yourself?" Kerry said to me in Afrikaans. The emphasis on his words was still off, his own Irish accent corrupting the natural intonations of the language, but I could understand him. It meant something more than I knew how to say that he had learnt my second tongue.

He patted at the cut with a paper towel and wrapped a small bandage around my finger, placing a light kiss on the back of my hand after sealing it tightly. That he kept a stash of bandages within reach in the kitchen was a testament to just how true his words were. I still couldn't cook like Kerry, but he'd taught me enough for me to make a passable Irish breakfast. And when I laid a plate of eggs, tomatoes and bacon in front of Kerry it always earned me a brilliant smile and a long kiss. Hence why I continued to brave bodily injury.

I turned to face him. "You look handsome," I said, putting my hands on his hips to draw him closer to me.

He scoffed. "I think I'm going to have to start dyeing my

hair."

Even though he'd only turned thirty-two a few weeks ago, Kerry was beginning to gray around his temples. The silver strands in his hair stood out against the black curls that he kept long now. I loved twining my hands in them, even if he just kept it long to avoid the gray being too obvious.

I told him that he deserved every gray hair. That he had earned them through his strength and perseverance. He said they made him look old.

I said distinguished.

He said decrepit.

I kissed him to silence him.

That always worked.

When we pulled away from each other I could hear his parents moving around upstairs.

"Are you ready for this?" I whispered.

"Aye."

I studied him, but I couldn't see any unease in his eyes. It had been a long time, years in fact, since I'd seen anything reminiscent of fear in Kerry. Ever since we'd returned to South Africa he was the Kerry I'd fallen in love with and yet not. His inherent innocence still surprised me some days, but he was stronger, much more sure of himself. There was a wisdom behind his eyes that for a while I had thought was sadness. Maybe that was what it was born out of, but it wasn't what he carried anymore. Kerry still saw the world, as Kelle had said, in ways that confounded me, but he talked to me about it now. Tried to explain his swirling thoughts. And I was getting better at taking a deep breath before I launched straight into frustration and anger.

I twisted the silver ring on my finger and thought about the moment Kerry had finally gotten the courage to ask me to marry him. At the time I'd been overwhelmed, shocked and happier than I'd ever been at any point in my life. But also terrified. I knew Kerry and I would always find our way back to each other, but I had to wonder what the next thing would be to pull us apart.

Because leaving each other was a skill Kerry and I had also mastered.

But something in our relationship shifted the day he stubbornly insisted on carrying me over the threshold of our house, even though it was going to be another year before we could legally get married. Blame the government for taking all the romance out of a spontaneous wedding.

It was as if we left the past at that door. The mistrust. The anger. The doubt.

I wish I could explain exactly why it seemed to work that way, but I no longer worried that we wouldn't be able to handle the hard times.

He told me that the last four years had changed him in ways he was still trying to understand, but that he trusted me to protect the last pieces of hope he still held onto.

We talked. A lot. Much more than men were supposed to talk. Or so I always thought. But that had been one of our problems all along.

We took time away from work and learnt about each other again. We spent hours with Abraham. We visited Kerry's parents in Ireland.

Then, after a month, we got back to the day-to-day business of running our company.

Before I knew it, it was five years later. And we were still together.

The years hadn't been easy. Our business had teetered on the edge of bankruptcy during the economic crash, but Kerry had had the idea to merge our company with the local great white conservation society and because of that move we'd been able to apply for grants that sustained us through the sparse years. With the merge, Abraham was back in the research business, and when I didn't have charters I was working with the staff on monitoring and protecting the sharks that traveled through our bay. When tourism started to pick up again we were in a better financial position than any of our competitors, and that was because of Kerry.

I circled my hand around his neck, running my fingers

through the curled ends at his nape, then pushed myself up by my tiptoes to give him a kiss on his cheek.

"And your parents?"

"They need this as much as we do. This is good, Erik. Really."

"I'm sorry. I don't mean to be overbearing. I know it's good. It's just going to be a tough day."

"For good reason. But also a happy day."

He nodded and smiled. "For good reason," I repeated. The warmth and surety in his smile filled me, calmed me. He was right. Today would be a happy day.

It had taken us four years to save and fundraise the entire amount, but today Great White Conservation Adventures would be christening the most modern ship in our fleet—a ship to be named the *Kelleigh Ann*. It was a sleek ship. Shiny, but not new. It was a fishing vessel salvaged from Thailand after the Indian Ocean Tsunami. The owner had been unable to afford the repairs. So I'd bought it off him for more than I should have paid, then had it towed back to Van Dyks Bay where Kerry had supervised its renovation. After salvage, towing, paint, materials and labor the ship had ended up costing more than it would have new.

But that wasn't the point.

Our new captain couldn't wait to take her out. I couldn't have convinced Mela to wait one more day.

"Give it a rest, you two. We know you're in love. And don't bleed into my eggs, yeah?" Mela teased. She had wanted to take the ship on a dive as soon as it was completed months ago, since we already had the permits, but Kerry wasn't having any of it. His parents couldn't make it out to South Africa until late December, so it only made sense to him that we hold the ceremony on December twenty-sixth, the sixth anniversary of the tsunami and days before our fifth wedding anniversary.

Next to her, Ed snickered.

Yes, even Ed was here, his massive *Trini's Passion II* in port farther up the coast because none of us could handle the behemoth ship at our docks, and his massive frame straining the chair at our dining room table. Trini was off at some meeting as usual, sending her regards. We didn't know any of the crew members left on the ship. Ed had a knack for driving them away. But he just kept sailing, completely oblivious to how oblivious he really was. Ever the *doff* I'd grown to love.

"Do we get to test out the new cage today too, Kerr?" Ed sipped at the cup of coffee in his hand, a mischievous glint in his eye, as Kerry took the seat next to Mela. While I'd lost touch with so many other supposed friends over the years, Ed always managed a call on my birthday and stopped by at least once a year to take a dive in our cage. And each time he would coax Kerry onto the boat with him despite Kerry's continued distrust of the sharks.

Kerry looked at me exasperated. "We! He says 'we' as if I have any real say in this."

"Well, I did travel all this way…"

Kerry rolled his eyes. Yet no matter how much Kerry protested, he would end up in a drysuit at Ed's side at some point today.

"Well, the captain of the new boat says we can do one short dive, but I want to take her out and see what she can do," Mela chastised us all.

"She's going to be a fast ship if she's anything like Kelle," Kerry's mum, Caroline, said, walking into the kitchen.

"And nimble," Kerry's dad Gerald added.

"And probably stubborn as fuck," Kerry mumbled under his breath and Mela cuffed him on the back of the head.

Caroline beamed as she poured herself a cup of coffee then laughed out loud when she noticed the bandage on my finger. "Attacked by the knife again, Erik?"

"Just come help me, please, before I take an entire finger off," I pleaded, even though I was holding a spatula.

She set her cup down and took the spatula to finish up the eggs, a grin plastered on her face. "Where's Abraham?" she asked over her shoulder as I started to fill plates.

172

"At the docks getting ready. He doesn't eat breakfast. Says that his family couldn't afford it growing up and he did just fine without it so he still refuses to eat it. Superstitious old man," I huffed.

Caroline pointed the spatula at me, but her tone was playful. "That superstitious old man is making sure you follow proper ship christening protocol. Give him a rest."

"Yes, ma'am," I replied with just a twitch of my lips.

"Don't be an arse," she laughed.

When we'd finished our breakfasts, Ed and Kerry ensuring every piece of bacon was gone before they were satisfied, Kerry and I cleaned up the kitchen while our guests talked about plans for New Year's Eve. The conversation was easy, amiable. And Kerry kept catching my eye as we moved around the tiny kitchen, his hand brushing my hip, solidifying the feeling of rightness humming softly in the background.

We stepped out the front door flanked by his parents, Mela and Ed behind us. By the cars lining the street, I had to assume that most of the city was already gathered around the docks. The sky was a light baby blue, reflected in the dark water that rolled lazily in the bay. There was only a soft wind today, pushing the waves onto the rocks with a muffled hush. The sun cut through the white wind-streaked clouds sliding in from the south, the rays washing over my skin until I could feel the warmth in my bones.

This was why I loved summertime in the Cape.

We walked around the new shop into a scene that was eerily reminiscent of the night of Kerry's birthday — the night of the fire. I expected to feel a sadness or at the very least a somberness to the entire event. But I couldn't have been more wrong. Abraham and Kerry had made the christening into a celebration. They had hung streamers from the shop down to the docks and each of our boats was covered in bright summertime flowers. We were greeted with wide smiles, laughter and congratulations.

This was our home. Our family. By blood, and by water.

I'd never felt more sure of who I was and what I was meant to do with my life. Or who I was meant to spend my life loving.

Abraham, Mela, Ed, Caroline, Gerald. Our crew and this town. The people who had stuck with us through the hard times.

But most importantly, Kerry.

The scene around us was so familiar and yet so different. Our lives had changed drastically since I'd first laid eyes on Kerry over twelve years ago. But I couldn't regret any of the decisions or events that had led us here because they had brought us to a place of understanding and peace.

That was when I almost lost it. Tears of joy mixed with sadness for those we had lost—my parents and uncle, Charlie, Kelleigh—started to spill down my cheeks. But Kerry wrapped his arm around my waist and, with a teasing whisper in my ear, told me that if Kelle had been here she would've told me to man up.

I laughed, because he was right.

Abraham made sure the appropriate words were said, and that each person held a glass in their hands to drink for the safety and health of those who brave the sea. I don't remember much of the speeches or the specifics of the official ceremony. But I will never forget the sheer joy on Caroline's and Gerald's faces when they smashed that oversized bottle of champagne against the hull of the *Kelleigh Ann* and it shattered into pieces, raining a foamy spray into the water as the crowd cheered.

I'll never forget Mela nearly jumping into my arms when I told her we could finally take her boat out to sea. I'll never forget Abraham patting my back and whispering congratulations in my ear, telling me how proud my parents and uncle would be of Kerry and me. Or Ed, bawling yet again, slobbering over Kerry and me when we stood on deck and felt the gentle roll of the ship below us.

And I'll never, ever, if I die one thousand years from now, be able to forget the calm strength of Kerry at my side. The way he couldn't suppress a smile any time someone said the name of the ship. The way his hand sought mine out over and over as the day turned to night and we eventually found ourselves alone, on the rocky beach in front of the shop, our friends and family stowed safely away in bedrooms across Van Dyks Bay.

"Do you think she would be proud or embarrassed?" I asked.

"You're joking, right? She would have hated this spectacle."

I chuckled. "And yet secretly loved it."

Kerry took my right hand in his, studying the silver rings we wore. The moonlight was just bright enough for me to see the tears welling in his eyes but not falling. He took a deep breath. "Which means we did her right."

I brought his hand to my lips and kissed his ring softly. "She would have been so proud of you."

We sat in silence so long that I decided it was time to go inside, but when I moved to stand Kerry tugged on my hand. He looked up at me, his green eyes shining. "I'm going with Mela to the prison next month," Kerry said so low I almost didn't hear him.

I wasn't surprised. I knew the drive to help someone else in need was too great for Kerry to ignore.

"He's all alone, Erik," Kerry said, as if he was begging me to understand.

I didn't understand. Not completely. But I knew why he felt as if he needed to do it, and I couldn't be mad at him for it. I nodded.

Kerry continued, "Fen was so young when they set that fire. So angry at himself. He was easily manipulated."

I patted his hand. "I know, Kerry."

Kerry shook his head. "It doesn't change what he did. That Charlie is dead because of him. And I don't know that I can ever forgive him for that. But I understand his fear."

I sighed. "It's the same fear you lived with for many years."

Kerry laughed darkly. "More than I care to count." He put his arm around my waist and pulled me to him. "But I had you to lead me through that fear. To see the other side. To know with complete certainty that I could be who I was and still be loved for it. I suppose I need for Fen to know that's possible for him too. Someday. Even here in Africa."

I wondered for a moment if he wanted me to go with him to the prison. I wasn't sure what I would answer if he did. But he never asked.

I looked off to the horizon where the blackened sky, overrun with stars, met the rolling waves of the ocean. The town around us was quiet, the only sound a soft lapping of waves on the rocks and the hulls of our boats.

I kissed his shoulder and leaned my head against him. "Thank you."

Kerry chuckled, the rumble from his chest passing through me in warm waves. "I would ask for what, but I already know."

"You do, yeah?"

"Aye. Because without me you'd be a stodgy old man obsessed with the sea. Grumpy."

I laughed. "Yeah. That's about right."

Kerry stood and pulled me with him. "Let's go to bed, old man."

And he kissed me. At first with just a brush of his lips then with an urgency that took my breath away, grasping onto me as if I was his lifeline. Although I knew the truth was more complicated than that.

We needed each other. Neither of us was complete without the other.

And we had the rest of our lives to show just how immoveable that love was.

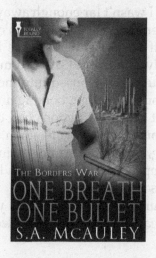

One Breath, One Bullet

Excerpt

Chapter One

Year 2546
The Dark Continental Republic

I hated the heat of the desert.

The mask on my face was confining, filling with the condensation of each breath I dragged into my lungs and forced back out in shallow gasps. The goggles over my eyes should have protected me from the yellow and grey cloud of Chemsense the Dark Continental Republic Army had unleashed on our battalion, but I could feel my eyes watering, the liquid gathering in pools that threatened to make my skin too damp to maintain the protective seal.

I was on my knees and I couldn't remember when I'd

stopped walking. I wasn't far enough away yet. The shouts of the DCR soldiers—and the sonicpops of their weapons as they picked off States soldiers—were muffled but still too close. My body tilted, and I planted my hands into the sand without thought. I collapsed into the dune when my right shoulder ground together, bone against bone, tendons ripping. I thought those DCR goons had only managed to dislocate it, but this pain was worse than that—a grinding impact of racking, vision-blackening pain that didn't ebb even when I flopped onto my back and let my arm lie unmoving in the scorching sand.

My mantra, pounded into me through years of training, repeated in my head as I consciously stilled my body.

One breath.

Inhale.

Hesitation is my enemy.

Solitude my ally.

Death the only real victory.

Exhale.

A ferocious hot wind whipped around and over me, driving sand into my open wounds, like a million simultaneous pricks of a pin. If the wind kept up like this it was going to drive away the lingering cloud of Chemsense. And I needed the thick, toxic cover if I was going to make it over the dune and out of sight of the DCR forces.

If I was going to survive, I had to keep moving.

My body was drenched in sweat—mine and the ripe remnants of the soldiers I'd fought hand to hand. My ribs on the right side were crushed and with each breath I wondered if this would be the inhalation that sent a spear of bone into the soft, vulnerable flesh of my lung, collapsing it and killing me before backup could arrive.

I ripped the transport chip out of the hidden pocket where it was sewed into my tattered uniform. My thumb hovered over the button as my mind warred with the instinct just to press it. But I couldn't simply transport out of this clusterfuck. The transition would be too much of a shock to my mangled body.

If I was going to succeed, I had to keep moving.

The thought was all that propelled me. There was no desire to survive left in me. No want of more from life. It was my orders, my mission, that forced me to sit up, shift to my knees and stumble to my feet.

My right arm hung loosely at my side. My firing arm. Without it I could never be a sniper again. And that should have been the least of my concerns, but I couldn't silence the part of me that contended that death would be preferential over never shooting my rifle again.

I staggered, then caught myself before falling again. The pain of my disconnected shoulder was almost too much to bear—a jolt of red, angry agony that sliced across my vision with each step forward. Silver droplets swam in my peripheral eyesight, a sign that my already throbbing head was on the verge of erupting.

I trudged through the unending sand of the DCR desert because I had no other choice. To stop was to fail. And I didn't fail. The sand felt thicker than the detritus of an American Federation riverbed. My feet sank deeper than into the suck of a United Union bog. I moved slower than the day I'd taken my first tentative steps off the hospital bed in the States when I was five years old and my legs had nearly been taken by the sonic explosion that had destroyed the only home I would ever know.

And I knew this desert was worse than all of those places because I was dying.

I was closer to death than I'd been in the People's Republic of Singapore the night Armise took a blade to my throat.

Armise.

The name rushed through me like endorphins, heating my already boiling blood. I barely had enough brain cells left active and firing to stand, let alone move, but my hate for Armise fed me like a vial of surge emptied into my bloodstream.

That I'd fucked him more times in the last year than I

wanted to count didn't matter.

That there had been a part of me anticipating he would be on the ground in the DCR when I arrived was like a psychotic practical joke.

He'd had the infochip I was seeking the entire time.

It had been inches from my fingers when I drove into him last night. But he had waited until my soldiers and me were trapped in a standoff with DCR forces — sonicrifle to sonicrifle — to let me in on that vital piece of intel.

I wouldn't let him so easily get under my skin again.

I might not have eliminated him, but I'd obtained the infochip I'd been sent to extract. And I'd taken Armise's finger in the process. I choked on the laughter that bubbled up in my throat. Too bad the missing digit wasn't on his firing hand.

If nothing else, I would survive to kill him.

Whatever this was between Armise and me ended here. Now.

But even in my haze I was aware of how irresolute that promise sounded.

I kept moving.

Until I wasn't anymore.

Blackness overtook me in an uncontrollable instant.

* * * *

There were snippets of fading consciousness. Voices, all male except one — floating, flying — how was that possible? — hands, caresses — water, fresh not treated — fingers poking, exploring, and I was unable to protest or question their invasion. My throat was on fire, my tongue thick, desert dry and swollen. Then the distinctive beep of a hand held medical sensor. More voices, never speaking directly to me. Then pain. Singeing, harrowing, mind-imploding torment. I tried to scream, but couldn't make a sound. My chest burned from the effort. My body arched off the table — bed? — and then someone was there, at my side, plunging a needle into the curve of my arm. The medicine—surge or something else?—was cool water dousing the fevered burn. Inch by soothing inch, the elixir travelled through me.

My vision swam as the medicine slammed into my consciousness and tried to drag me under. I fought to keep my eyes open, to see where I was and with whom. I no longer wore my goggles or my respirator. The air I dragged in between my parched lips was clean, free of the sickly sweet tinge of Chemsense or the choking thickness of urban pollution. I didn't know if I was a prisoner or among allies, but I had to assume I was still in the DCR.

The room was dark. The wooden walls appeared to bend and twist and then I realised it was my eyes that were moving, not the room. I didn't know how much of what I was seeing was reality. Figures moved around where I lay, calming hands, hunched shoulders, unintelligible whispers and a cool brush of cloth across my forehead.

Thank you, I had the urge to say. But no sound came out.

A hand on my head, the graze of a coarser fabric on my cooling skin, and my eyes started to close.

Then the wet rag was gone and I saw a bandaged left hand pull away, the fifth finger missing, and I knew for certain that I was hallucinating.

I let myself slip into the darkness again.

* * * *

When I woke up I was alone in a white tiled room, the distinctive high of surge blasting through my veins. I was more than awake. I was alive—whole, I could feel the strength in the tension of my muscles—and immediately antsy. The need to move was palpable. I scanned the room. I was in a bed, wires and tubes snaking from my arms, which were pinned to the bed with beige cloth straps. Under the white blanket that covered me I moved my feet. They were tethered as well.

I wasn't in the DCR anymore, of that I could be sure. Only the States had medical facilities this advanced.

Which meant that somehow I'd made it back home.

I struggled against the bindings holding me to the bed and a man appeared at my side. I remembered his face but not his name. A doctor for the States. I'd seen him before for routine physicals. He was the one who had stitched Jegs' slashed face back together after her rescue in Singapore.

I stopped fighting the restraints when the doctor stepped back from the bed and eyed me. I swallowed and cleared my throat.

"How long?" I croaked out. My voice was thick, it took effort to push the words from my lungs, up my throat and out of my mouth, as if I hadn't spoken in a long time.

The doctor worked at the bindings on one side then the other until my arms were free. "We've had you under for almost two months. We repaired your shoulder and ribs as thoroughly as possible. We tried to give you titanalloy ribs, but your body rejected the material quite severely. Regardless, they're also healed by now." He moved to my feet, throwing off the blanket and undoing the restraints there. "I wanted to remove your entire right arm and give you a synth, but Neveed refused to let me take it off."

I glared at the doctor and tried to sit up. Synthetic limbs, synths for short, were commonplace but having one would have eliminated me from active duty. At least someone had been thinking about the long term when I'd ended up here.

Two months. I'd been out for two months.

I ran my fingers through my brown hair. It was longer now. Not the shave job I'd had done for my mission in the blistering heat of the DCR. I moved my hands over my eyebrow, my lip and the shell of my left ear, counting the hoops and studs. All of my piercings remained. That, too, was probably the work of Coach.

"How many made it out?" I asked as the harsh reality of my situation settled in.

The doctor shook his head. "Only you."

I cringed. Fuck. Over one hundred Peacemakers had gone into that village. But I was used to losing soldiers. It happened every mission. This particular mission had one goal though, and it was the battalion's job to make sure I achieved it.

"Who has the infochip?" I asked.

The doctor's face went blank. Unreadable. "I don't know," he replied, and I could tell his answer was a lie.

I ground my teeth together. If all those soldiers had died and I hadn't made it out with that chip I was going to have hell to pay. "It did come with me, right?"

The doctor started removing the wires from my arm. "It's here. But you didn't hear that from me. Now sit still. I know you want to move. That's normal. But you're not getting out of this bed unless you comply."

I narrowed my eyes at him and held out my left arm, pleased to see it didn't shake with the effort to hold it still. "What else do you know?"

The doctor pulled the IV needle free from the crook of my arm and put a bandage over the drop of blood that appeared. He crossed his arms and stepped back from the table. "You're going to have to talk to Neveed."

I snorted. Yeah, right. Coach was the last person I wanted to talk to after sending me to that hellhole that I'd barely survived.

"How did I get here?"

"Can't answer that one either. A whole lot about you is classified."

I lifted my right arm, testing my strength. I'd definitely lost muscle mass but that would be easy to replace. Months at the most to regain my full strength. It would have taken years for me to adjust to a synth.

"Go ahead," the doctor instructed. "Rotate it around. Your shoulder is not going to be as strong as you remember. It was too badly damaged and you were away from care for too long. But I think you will see an almost full recovery. Not that it matters quite as much as anymore. They have called a truce."

My eyes met his. "To the war?"

The doctor frowned. "What else is there?"

I shook my head and dismissed him with a wave.

That the Borders War had been waged for three hundred years and was finally over was of little consequence to me. I knew there would be celebration – a citizenry grateful to its leaders for ending the strife that had wiped four hundred million people from the planet. But their joy was premature. Unfounded.

I steeled myself. It didn't matter whether the Borders War was over or not. My mission, the one I'd been preparing for my entire life, hadn't ended with my acquisition of the infochip. It wouldn't end with a truce. And whether anyone wanted to believe it or not, I knew the real war was only beginning.

* * * *

It was another two years before active combat finally stopped.

The world was in the midst of a tenuous peace. After three centuries of brutal fighting, and the territorial lines of our world under constant shifts, the treaty – signed by the five leaders in the crumbling parliamentary building of the United Union – was hesitant at best. Fury still simmered just below the surface.

With peace came more strife. This time in the rebuilding. In the awakening that was the aftermath. As if the world was collectively blinking the dust from their eyes, seeing their existence for the hell it was and finally realising how inequitable our society had become. An undying will to break free was barely restrained by the governments of the five countries that had been the victors in the end – if anyone could actually be called victorious in a war that had wiped out half of the world's population.

I was just one lightning strike in the gathering storm.

In the time since the States had gained possession of the infochip I'd nearly lost my life over, the encryption hadn't been broken.

The information it was fabled to contain couldn't be verified, let alone studied. And it was these details that were coveted by every government.

So my superiors sent me after the only man who could be definitively tied to it.

Armise didn't seem surprised to see me.

Maybe it was because he was in Bogotá. Of all the places in the world, he had to be in the city where I'd first met him.

The city was different than the last time I'd been here. No longer as war-torn, no longer as destroyed. There were signs of rebuilding. The American Federation had emerged from the war stronger than anyone had anticipated.

I remembered a Bogotá of crumbling ancient architecture. But Armise sat in a cafe that could only be called modern and genteel. Wire tables and chairs outside of a low angular metal building. A glass vase of spring flowers sat in the centre of the table. Armise was sipping from a white cup that looked ridiculous in his massive hands. But even that couldn't belie his aura of power.

Passersby gave Armise a wide berth for good reason. The man's inscrutable face was scarred with marks that ran across his temple, and down his cheek. There were slashes on his jaw and neck I had given him. Then other marks I only knew the stories about from classified files. His frame was mammoth in comparison to the diminutive thinness of the citizens surrounding him. In the distance, the mountains surrounding the city towered high above the cranes that projected from the skyline.

His left hand lay on the table, that missing fifth digit a reminder that should have brought disturbing and angry memories to the forefront, but instead made my lip twitch in a smirk.

He wasn't yet thirty years old but silver streaked from his temples. He wore a plain grey sweater against the lingering chill of winter. It clung to him. To his broad shoulders. He was bigger than I remembered, as if time had attempted to diminish him in my memory.

Bogotá was a cloud-covered city that rarely saw sunshine, but the sun blazed in the sky, dissipating the pollution haze that hovered above every major city touched by war. I was sure the only reason for the blinding brightness was to mock me. Because I shouldn't have felt as drawn to Armise as I was walking to that table.

The feet of the chair screeched on the concrete as I pulled it out and settled across from him. My expression was flat, disinterested, when every nerve in my body was on edge. Armise was just as outwardly calm. Which was normal. And it shouldn't have mattered that I knew that, but it did.

"Missed me?" Armise said, breaking the silence between us, a sly grin spreading across his face.

I sneered.

Armise hummed in response and sat back in his chair. "Yeah, me too."

"I'd prefer to get right to the point. Since our last meeting was so eventful," I dryly answered.

Armise tapped the fingers of his left hand on the silver wire table. I didn't acknowledge his recognition of what had occurred the last time we encountered each other. "And the point is?"

"The encryption key for the infochip." I wasn't going to play head games with Armise. Being this close to him, able to smell the exotic mix of Singaporean balms he used to ease his muscles, was already affecting me.

Armise crossed his arms. If my presence was having any effect on him he didn't show it. "Obtaining the key became your problem when you and your supposed Peacemakers decided to barge in on my deal."

More books from
S.A. McAuley

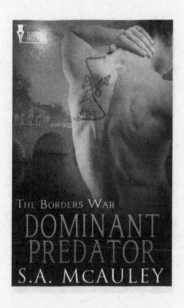

*A relationship is the least of Merq and Armise's
concerns…*

More books from

S.A. McAuley

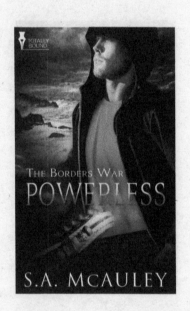

He was built to be invincible.

THE BORDERS WAR

They've spent fifteen years living on the knife's edge of trust and loyalty

FALLING,
ONE BY ONE
S.A. McAULEY

Whether Armise lived or died was never supposed to matter to Merq.

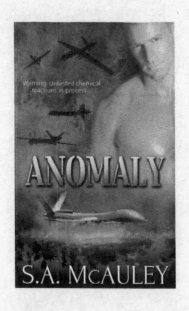

Warning: Untested chemical reactions in process…

About the Author

S.A. McAuley

I sleep little, read a lot. Happiest in a foreign country. Twitchy when not mentally in motion. My name is Sam, not Sammy, definitely not Samantha. I'm a pretty dark/cynical/jaded person, but I hide that darkness well behind my obsession(s) for shiny objects. I'm the macabre wrapped in irresistible bubble wrap and a glittery pink bow, I suppose.

S.A. McAuley loves to hear from readers. You can find contact information, website details and an author profile page at https://www.pride-publishing.com/

PRIDE

PUBLISHING